*Ten Classic Crime Stories
for the Festive Season*

MURDER
UNDER THE
CHRISTMAS TREE

Edited by Cecily Gayford

*Ian Rankin · Dorothy L. Sayers
Margery Allingham · Arthur Conan Doyle
Val McDermid · Ellis Peters · Edmund Crispin
G. K. Chesterton · Ngaio Marsh
Carter Dickson*

P

PROFILE BOOKS

First published in Great Britain in 2016 by
PROFILE BOOKS LTD
3 Holford Yard
Bevin Way
London WC1X 9HD
www.profilebooks.com

Chosen and edited by Cecily Gayford
Selection copyright © Profile Books Ltd, 2016

3 5 7 9 10 8 6 4

Typeset in Fournier by MacGuru Ltd
Printed and bound in Great Britain by CPI Group (UK) Ltd, Croydon CR0 4YY

A CIP catalogue record for this book is available from the British Library.

ISBN 978 1 78125 791 3
eISBN 978 1 78283 332 1

MURDER
UNDER THE
CHRISTMAS TREE

Contents

The Necklace of Pearls

Dorothy L. Sayers

Sir Septimus Shale was accustomed to assert his authority once in the year and once only. He allowed his young and fashionable wife to fill his house with diagrammatic furniture made of steel; to collect advanced artists and anti-grammatical poets; to believe in cocktails and relativity and to dress as extravagantly as she pleased; but he did insist on an old-fashioned Christmas. He was a simple-hearted man, who really liked plum-pudding and cracker mottoes, and he could not get it out of his head that other people, 'at bottom,' enjoyed these things also. At Christmas, therefore, he firmly retired to his country house in Essex, called in the servants to hang holly and mistletoe upon the cubist electric fittings; loaded the steel sideboard with delicacies from Fortnum & Mason; hung up stockings at the heads of the polished walnut bed-steads; and even, on this occasion only, had the electric radiators removed from the modernist grates and installed wood fires and a Yule log. He then gathered his family and friends about him, filled them with as much Dickensian good fare as he could persuade them to swallow, and, after their Christmas dinner, set them down to play 'Charades' and 'Clumps' and 'Animal, Vegetable, and Mineral' in the drawing-room, concluding these diversions by 'Hide-and-Seek' in the dark all over the house. Because Sir Septimus was a very rich man, his guests fell in with this invariable programme, and if they were bored, they did not tell him so.

Another charming and traditional custom which he followed was that of presenting to his daughter Margharita a pearl on each successive birthday – this anniversary happening to coincide with Christmas Eve. The pearls now numbered twenty, and the collection was beginning to enjoy a certain celebrity, and had been photographed in the Society papers. Though not sensationally large – each one being about the size of a marrow-fat pea – the pearls were of very great value. They were of exquisite colour and perfect shape and matched to a hair's-weight. On this particular Christmas Eve, the presentation of the twenty-first pearl had been the occasion of a very special ceremony. There was a dance and there were speeches.

On the Christmas night following, the more restricted family party took place, with the turkey and the Victorian games. There were eleven guests, in addition to Sir Septimus and Lady Shale and their daughter, nearly all related or connected to them in some way: John Shale, a brother with his wife and their son and daughter Henry and Betty; Betty's fiancé, Oswald Truegood, a young man with parliamentary ambitions; George Comphrey, a cousin of Lady Shale's, aged about thirty and known as a man about town; Lavinia Prescott, asked on George's account; Joyce Trivett, asked on Henry Shale's account; Richard and Beryl Dennison, distant relations of Lady Shale, who lived a gay and expensive life in town on nobody precisely knew what resources; and Lord Peter Wimsey, asked, in a touching spirit of unreasonable hope, on Margharita's account. There were also, of course, William Norgate, secretary to Sir Septimus, and Miss Tomkins, secretary to Lady Shale, who had to be there because, without their calm efficiency, the Christmas arrangements could not have been carried through.

Dinner was over – a seemingly endless succession of soup, fish, turkey, roast beef, plum-pudding, mince-pies, crystallized fruit, nuts, and five kinds of wine, presided over by Sir Septimus, all smiles, by Lady Shale, all mocking deprecation, and by Margharita, pretty and bored, with the necklace of twenty-one pearls gleaming softly on her slender throat. Gorged and dyspeptic and longing only for the horizontal position, the company had been shepherded into the drawing-room and set to play 'Musical Chairs' (Miss Tomkins at the piano), 'Hunt the Slipper' (slipper provided by Miss Tomkins), and 'Dumb Crambo' (costumes by Miss Tomkins and Mr William Norgate). The back drawing-room (for Sir Septimus clung to these old-fashioned names) provided an admirable dressing-room, being screened by folding doors from the large drawing-room in which the audience sat on aluminum chairs, scrabbling uneasy toes on a floor of black glass under the tremendous illumination of electricity reflected from a brass ceiling.

It was William Norgate who, after taking the temperature of the meeting, suggested to Lady Shale that they should play at something less athletic. Lady Shale agreed and, as usual, suggested bridge. Sir Septimus, as usual, blew the suggestion aside.

'Bridge? Nonsense! Nonsense! Play bridge every day of your lives. This is Christmas time. Something we can all play together. How about "Animal, Vegetable, and Mineral"?'

This intellectual pastime was a favourite with Sir Septimus; he was rather good at putting pregnant questions. After a brief discussion, it became evident that this game was an inevitable part of the programme. The party settled down to it, Sir Septimus undertaking to 'go out' first and set the thing going.

Presently they had guessed among other things Miss Tomkins's mother's photograph, a gramophone record of 'I want to be happy' (much scientific research into the exact composition of records, settled by William Norgate out of the *Encyclopaedia Britannica*), the smallest stickle-back in the stream at the bottom of the garden, the new planet Pluto, the scarf worn by Mrs Dennison (very con-fusing, because it was not silk, which would be animal, or artificial silk, which would be vegetable, but made of spun glass – mineral, a very clever choice of subject), and had failed to guess the Prime Minister's wireless speech – which was voted not fair, since nobody could decide whether it was animal by nature or a kind of gas. It was decided that they should do one more word and then go on to 'Hide-and-Seek'. Oswald Truegood had retired into the back room and shut the door behind him while the party discussed the next subject of examination, when suddenly Sir Septimus broke in on the argument by calling to his daughter:

'Hullo, Margy! What have you done with your necklace?'

'I took it off, Dad, because I thought it might get broken in "Dumb Crambo". It's over here on this table. No, it isn't. Did you take it, mother?'

'No, I didn't. If I'd seen it, I should have. You are a careless child.'

'I believe you've got it yourself, Dad. You're teasing.'

Sir Septimus denied the accusation with some energy. Everybody got up and began to hunt about. There were not many places in that bare and polished room where a necklace could be hidden. After ten minutes' fruitless investigation, Richard Dennison, who had been seated next to the table where the pearls had been placed, began to look rather uncomfortable.

'Awkward, you know,' he remarked to Wimsey.

At this moment, Oswald Truegood put his head through the folding-doors and asked whether they hadn't settled on something by now, because he was getting the fidgets.

This directed the attention of the searchers to the inner room. Margharita must have been mistaken. She had taken it in there, and it had got mixed up with the dressing-up clothes somehow. The room was ransacked. Everything was lifted up and shaken. The thing began to look serious. After half an hour of desperate energy it became apparent that the pearls were nowhere to be found.

'They must be somewhere in these two rooms, you know,' said Wimsey. 'The back drawing-room has no door and nobody could have gone out of the front drawing-room without being seen. Unless the windows—'

No. The windows were all guarded on the outside by

heavy shutters which it needed two footmen to take down and replace. The pearls had not gone out that way. In fact, the mere suggestion that they had left the drawing-room at all was disagreeable. Because – because –

It was William Norgate, efficient as ever, who coldly and boldly faced the issue.

'I think, Sir Septimus, it would be a relief to the minds of everybody present if we could all be searched.'

Sir Septimus was horrified, but the guests, having found a leader, backed up Norgate. The door was locked, and the search was conducted – the ladies in the inner room and the men in the outer.

Nothing resulted from it except some very interesting information about the belongings habitually carried about by the average man and woman. It was natural that Lord Peter Wimsey should possess a pair of forceps, a pocket lens, and a small folding foot-rule – was he not a Sherlock Holmes in high life? But that Oswald Truegood should have two liver-pills in a screw of paper and Henry Shale a pocket edition of *The Odes of Horace* was unexpected. Why did John Shale distend the pockets of his dress-suit with a stump of red sealing-wax, an ugly little mascot, and a five-shilling piece? George Comphrey had a pair of folding scissors, and three wrapped lumps of sugar, of the sort served in restaurants and dining-cars – evidence of a not uncommon form of kleptomania; but that the tidy and exact Norgate should burden himself with a reel of white cotton, three separate lengths of string, and twelve safety-pins on a card seemed really remarkable till one remembered that he had superintended all the Christmas decorations. Richard Dennison, amid some confusion and laughter, was found to cherish a lady's garter, a powder-compact, and half a potato; the last-named, he said, was a prophylactic against rheumatism (to which he was subject), while the other objects belonged to his wife. On the ladies' side, the more striking exhibits were a little book on palmistry, three invisible hair-pins, and a baby's photograph (Miss Tomkins); a Chinese trick cigarette-case with a secret compartment (Beryl Dennison); a *very* private letter and an outfit for mending stocking-ladders (Lavinia Prescott); and a pair of eyebrow tweezers and a small packet of white powder, said to be for headaches (Betty Shale). An agitating moment followed the production from Joyce Trivett's handbag of a small string of pearls – but it was promptly remembered that these had come out of one of the crackers at dinnertime, and they were, in fact, synthetic. In short, the search was unproductive of anything beyond a general shamefacedness and the discomfort always produced by undressing and re-dressing in a hurry at the wrong time of the day.

It was then that somebody, very grudgingly and haltingly, mentioned the horrid word 'Police.' Sir Septimus, naturally, was appalled by the idea. It was disgusting. He would not allow it. The pearls must be somewhere. They must search the rooms again. Could not Lord Peter Wimsey, with his experience of – er – mysterious happenings, do something to assist them?

'Eh?' said his lordship. 'Oh, by Jove, yes – by all means, certainly. That is to say, provided nobody supposes – eh, what? I mean to say, you don't know that I'm not a suspicious character, do you, what?'

Lady Shale interposed with authority.

'We don't think *anybody* ought to be suspected,' she said, 'but, if we did, we'd know it couldn't be you. You know *far* too much about crimes to want to commit one.'

'All right,' said Wimsey. 'But after the way the place has been gone over – ' He shrugged his shoulders.

'Yes, I'm afraid you won't be able to find any footprints,' said Margharita. 'But we may have overlooked something.'

Wimsey nodded.

'I'll try. Do you all mind sitting down on your chairs in the outer room and staying there. All except one of you – I'd better have a witness to anything I do or find. Sir Septimus – you'd be the best person, I think.'

He shepherded them to their places and began a slow circuit of the two rooms, exploring every surface, gazing up to the polished brazen ceiling, and crawling on hands and knees in the approved fashion across the black and shining desert of the floors. Sir Septimus followed, staring when Wimsey stared, bending with his hands upon his knees when Wimsey crawled, and puffing at intervals with astonishment and chagrin. Their progress rather resembled that of a man taking out a very inquisitive puppy for a very leisurely constitutional. Fortunately, Lady Shale's taste in furnishing made investigation easier; there were scarcely any nooks or corners where anything could be concealed.

They reached the inner drawing-room, and here the dressing-up clothes were again minutely examined, but without result. Finally, Wimsey lay down flat on his stomach to squint under a steel cabinet which was one of the very few pieces of furniture which possessed short legs. Something about it seemed to catch his attention. He rolled up his sleeve and plunged his arm into the cavity, kicked convulsively in the effort to reach farther than was humanly possible, pulled out from his pocket and extended his folding foot-rule, fished with it under the cabinet, and eventually succeeded in extracting what he sought.

It was a very minute object – in fact, a pin. Not an ordinary pin, but one resembling those used by entomologists to impale extremely small moths on the setting-board. It was about three-quarters of an inch in length, as fine as a very fine needle, with a sharp point and a particularly small head.

'Bless my soul!' said Sir Septimus. 'What's that?'

'Does anybody here happen to collect moths or beetles or anything?' asked Wimsey, squatting on his haunches and examining the pin.

'I'm pretty sure they don't,' replied Sir Septimus. 'I'll ask them.'

'Don't do that.' Wimsey bent his head and stared at the floor, from which his own face stared meditatively back at him.

'I see,' said Wimsey presently. 'That's how it was done. All right, Sir Septimus. I know where the pearls are, but I don't know who took them. Perhaps it would be as well – for everybody's satisfaction – just to find out. In the meantime they are perfectly safe. Don't tell anyone that we've found this pin or that we've discovered anything. Send all these people to bed. Lock the drawing-room door and keep the key, and we'll get our man – or woman – by breakfast-time.'

'God bless my soul,' said Sir Septimus, very much puzzled.

Lord Peter Wimsey kept careful watch that night upon the drawing-room door. Nobody, however, came near it. Either the thief suspected a trap or he felt confident that any time would do to recover the pearls. Wimsey, however, did not feel that he was wasting his time. He was making a list of people who had been left alone in the back drawing-room during the playing of 'Animal, Vegetable, and Mineral.' The list ran as follows:

Sir Septimus Shale
Lavinia Prescott
William Norgate
Joyce Trivett and Henry Shale (together, because
they had claimed to be incapable of guessing anything
unaided)
Mrs Dennison
Betty Shale
George Comphrey
Richard Dennison
Miss Tomkins
Oswald Truegood

He also made out a list of the persons to whom pearls might be useful or desirable. Unfortunately, this list agreed in almost all respects with the first (always excepting Sir Septimus) and so was not very helpful. The two secretaries had both come well recommended, but that was exactly what they would have done had they come with ulterior designs; the Dennisons were notorious livers from hand to mouth; Betty Shale carried mysterious white powders in her handbag, and was known to be in with a rather rapid set in town; Henry was a harmless dilettante, but Joyce

Trivett could twist him round her little finger and was what Jane Austen liked to call 'expensive and dissipated'; Comphrey speculated; Oswald Truegood was rather frequently present at Epsom and Newmarket – the search for motives was only too fatally easy.

When the second housemaid and the under-footman appeared in the passage with household implements, Wimsey abandoned his vigil, but he was down early to breakfast Sir Septimus with his wife and daughter were down before him, and a certain air of tension made itself felt. Wimsey, standing on the hearth before the fire, made conversation about the weather and politics.

The party assembled gradually, but, as though by common consent, nothing was said about pearls until after breakfast, when Oswald Truegood took the bull by the horns.

'Well now!' said he. 'How's the detective getting along? Got your man, Wimsey?'

'Not yet,' said Wimsey easily.

Sir Septimus, looking at Wimsey as though for his cue, cleared his throat and dashed into speech.

'All very tiresome,' he said, 'all very unpleasant. Hr'rm. Nothing for it but the police, I'm afraid. Just at Christmas, too. Hr'rm. Spoilt the party. Can't stand seeing all this stuff about the place.' He waved his hand towards the festoons of evergreens and coloured paper that adorned the walls. 'Take it all down, eh, what? No heart in it. Hr'rm. Burn the lot.'

'What a pity, when we worked so hard over it,' said Joyce.

'Oh, leave it, Uncle,' said Henry Shale. 'You're bothering too much about the pearls. They're sure to turn up.'

'Shall I ring for James?' suggested William Norgate.

'No,' interrupted Comphrey, 'let's do it ourselves. It'll give us something to do and take our minds off our troubles.'

'That's right,' said Sir Septimus. 'Start right away. Hate the sight of it.'

He savagely hauled a great branch of holly down from the mantelpiece and flung it, crackling, into the fire.

'That's the stuff,' said Richard Dennison. 'Make a good old blaze!' He leapt up from the table and snatched the mistletoe from the chandelier. 'Here goes! One more kiss for somebody before it's too late.'

'Isn't it unlucky to take it down before the New Year?' suggested Miss Tomkins.

'Unlucky be hanged. We'll have it all down. Off the stairs and out of the drawing-room too. Somebody go and collect it.'

'Isn't the drawing-room locked?' asked Oswald.

'No. Lord Peter says the pearls aren't there, wherever else they are, so it's unlocked. That's right, isn't it, Wimsey?'

'Quite right. The pearls were taken out of these rooms. I can't tell yet how, but I'm positive of it. In fact, I'll pledge my reputation that wherever they are, they're not up there.'

'Oh, well,' said Comphrey, 'in that case, have at it! Come along, Lavinia – you and Dennison do the drawing-room and I'll do the back room. We'll have a race.'

'But if the police are coming in,' said Dennison, 'oughtn't everything to be left just as it is?'

'Damn the police!' shouted Sir Septimus. 'They don't want evergreens.'

Oswald and Margharita were already pulling the holly and ivy from the staircase, amid peals of laughter. The party dispersed. Wimsey went quietly upstairs and into the drawing-room, where the work of demolition was taking place at a great rate, George having bet the other two ten shillings to a tanner that they would not finish their part of the job before he finished his.

'You mustn't help,' said Lavinia, laughing to Wimsey. 'It wouldn't be fair.'

Wimsey said nothing, but waited till the room was clear. Then he followed them down again to the hall, where the fire was sending up a great roaring and splut-tering, suggestive of Guy Fawkes' night. He whispered to Sir Septimus, who went forward and touched George Comphrey on the shoulder.

'Lord Peter wants to say something to you, my boy,' he said.

Comphrey started and went with him a little reluctantly, as it seemed. He was not looking very well.

'Mr Comphrey,' said Wimsey, 'I fancy these are some of your property.' He held out the palm of his hand, in which rested twenty-two fine, small-headed pins.

'Ingenious,' said Wimsey, 'but something less ingenious would have served his turn better. It was very unlucky, Sir Septimus, that you should have mentioned the pearls when you did. Of course, he hoped that the loss wouldn't be discovered till we'd chucked guessing games and taken to "Hide-and-Seek". Then the pearls might have been anywhere in the house, we shouldn't have locked the drawing-room door, and he could have recovered them at his leisure. He had had this possibility in his mind when he came here, obviously, and that was why he brought the pins, and Miss Shale's taking off the necklace to play "Dumb Crambo" gave him his opportunity.

'He had spent Christmas here before, and knew perfectly well that "Animal, Vegetable, and Mineral" would form part of the entertainment. He had only to gather up the necklace from the table when it came to his turn to retire, and he knew he could count on at least five minutes by himself while we were all arguing about the choice of a word. He had only to snip the pearls from the string with his pocket-scissors, burn the string in the grate, and fasten the pearls to the mistletoe with the fine pins. The mistletoe was hung on the chandelier, pretty high – it's a lofty room – but he could easily reach it by standing on the glass table, which wouldn't show footmarks, and it was almost certain that nobody would think of examining the mistletoe for extra berries. I shouldn't have thought of it myself if I hadn't found that pin which he had dropped. That gave me the idea that the pearls had been separated and the rest was easy. I took the pearls off the mistletoe last night – the clasp was there, too, pinned among the holly-leaves. Here they are. Comphrey must have got a nasty shock this morning. I knew he was our man when he suggested that the guests should tackle the decorations themselves and that he should do the back drawing-room – but I wish I had seen his face when he came to the mistletoe and found the pearls gone.'

'And you worked it all out when you found the pin?' said Sir Septimus.

'Yes; I knew then where the pearls had gone to.' 'But you never even looked at the mistletoe.' 'I saw it reflected in the black glass floor, and it struck me then how much the mistletoe berries looked like pearls.'

The Name on the Window

Edmund Crispin

Boxing Day; snow and ice; road-surfaces like glass under a cold fog. In the North Oxford home of the University Professor of English Language and Literature, at three minutes past seven in the evening, the front door bell rang.

The current festive season had taken heavy toll of Fen's vitality and patience; it had culminated, that afternoon, in a quite exceptionally tiring children's party, amid whose ruins he was now recouping his energies with whisky; and on hearing the bell he jumped inevitably to the conclusion that one of the infants he had bundled out of the door half an hour previously had left behind it some such prized inessential as a false nose or a bachelors button, and was returning to claim this. In the event, however, and despite his premonitory groans, this assumption proved to be incorrect: his doorstep was occupied, he found, not by a dyspeptic, over-heated child with an unintelligible query, but by a neatly dressed greying man with a red tip to his nose and woebegone eyes.

'I can't get back,' said this apparition. 'I really can't get back to London tonight. The roads are impassable and such trains as there are are running hours late. Could you possibly let me have a bed?'

The tones were familiar; and by peering more attentively at the face, Fen discovered that that was familiar too. 'My dear Humbleby,' he said cordially, 'do come in. Of course you can have a bed. What are you doing in this part of the world, anyway?'

'Ghost-hunting.' Detective Inspector Humbleby, of New Scotland Yard, divested himself of his coat and hat and hung them on a hook inside the door. 'Seasonable but not convenient.' He stamped his feet violently, thereby producing, to judge from his expression, sensations of pain rather than of warmth; and stared about him. '*Children*,' he said with sudden gloom. 'I dare say that one of the Oxford hotels – '

'The children have left,' Fen explained, 'and will not be coming back.'

'Ah. Well, in that case –' And Humbleby followed Fen into the drawing-room, where a huge fire was burning and a slightly lop-sided Christmas tree, stripped of its treasures, wore tinsel and miniature witch-balls and a superincumbent fairy with a raffish air. 'My word, this is better. Is there a drink, perhaps? I could do with some advice, too.'

Fen was already pouring whisky. 'Sit down and be comfortable,' he said. 'As a matter of interest, do you believe in ghosts?'

'The evidence *for poltergeists,*' Humbleby answered warily as he stretched out his hands to the blaze, 'seems very convincing to me…. The Wesleys, you know, and Harry Price and so forth. Other sorts of ghosts I'm not so sure about – though I must say I *hope* they exist, if only for the purpose of taking that silly grin off the faces of the newspapers.' He picked up a battered tin locomotive from beside him on the sofa. 'I say, Gervase, I was under the impression that your own children were all too old for –'

'Orphans,' said Fen, jabbing at the siphon. 'I've been entertaining orphans from a nearby Home…. But as regards this particular ghost you were speaking of –'

'Oh, I don't believe in *that.*' Humbleby shook his head decisively. 'There's an obscure sort of nastiness about the place it's supposed to haunt – like a very sickly cake gone stale – and a man *was* killed there once, by a girl he was trying to persuade to certain practices she didn't relish at all; but the haunting part of it is just silly gossip for the benefit of visitors.' Humbleby accepted the glass which Fen held out to him and brooded over it for a moment before drinking. '... Damned Chief Inspector,' he muttered aggrievedly, 'dragging me away from my Christmas lunch because –'

'Really, Humbleby' – Fen was severe – 'you're very inconsequent this evening. Where is this place you're speaking of?'

'Rydalls.'

'Rydalls?'

'Rydalls,' said Humbleby. 'The residence,' he elucidated laboriously, 'of Sir Charles Moberley, the architect. It's about fifteen miles from here, Abingdon way.'

'Yes, I remember it now. Restoration.'

'I dare say. Old, in any case. And there are big grounds, with an eighteenth-century pavilion about a quarter of a mile away from the house, in a park. That's where it happened – the murder, I mean.'

'The murder of the man who tried to induce the girl –'

'No, no. I mean, yes. *That* murder took place in the pavilion, certainly. But then, so did the other one – the one the day before yesterday, that's to say.'

Fen stared. 'Sir Charles Moberley has been murdered?'

'No, no, no. Not *him*. Another architect, another knight

– Sir Lucas Welsh. There's been quite a large house party going on at Rydalls, with Sir Lucas Welsh and his daughter Jane among the guests, and it was on Christmas Eve, you see, that Sir Lucas decided he wanted to investigate the ghost.'

'This is all clear enough to you, no doubt, but – '

'Do *listen*... It seems that Sir Lucas is – was – credulous about ghosts, so on Christmas Eve he arranged to keep vigil alone in the pavilion and – '

'And was murdered, and you don't know who did it.'

'Oh yes, I do. Sir Lucas didn't die at once, you see: he had time to write up his murderer's name in the grime of the window-pane, and the gentleman concerned, a young German named Otto Mörike, is now safely under arrest. But what I can't decide is how Mörike got in and out of the pavilion.'

'A locked-room mystery.'

'In the wider sense, just that. The pavilion wasn't actually locked, but – '

Fen collected his glass from the mantelpiece, where he had put it on rising to answer the door-bell. 'Begin,' he suggested, 'at the beginning.'

'Very well.' Settling back in the sofa, Humbleby sipped his whisky gratefully. 'Here, then, is this Christmas house party at Rydalls. Host, Sir Charles Moberley, the eminent architect.... Have you ever come across him?'

Fen shook his head.

'A big man, going grey: in some ways rather boisterous and silly, like a rugger-playing medical student in a state of arrested development. Unmarried; private means – quite a lot of them, to judge from the sort of hospitality he dispenses; did the Wandsworth power-station and Beckford Abbey, among other things; athlete; a simple mind, and generous, I should judge, in that jealous sort of way which resents generosity in anyone else. Probably tricky, in some respects – he's not the kind of person *I* could ever feel completely at ease with.

'A celebrity, however: unquestionably that. And Sir Lucas Welsh, whom among others he invited to this house party, was equally a celebrity, in the same line of business. Never having seen Sir Lucas alive, I can't say much about his character, but – '

'I think,' Fen interrupted, 'that I may have met him once, at the time when he was designing the fourth quadrangle for my college. A small dark person, wasn't he?'

'Yes, that's right.'

'And with a tendency to be nervy and obstinate.'

'The obstinacy there's evidence for, certainly. And I gather he was also a good deal of a faddist – Yogi, I mean, and the Baconian hypothesis, and a lot of other intellectual – um – detritus of the same dull, obvious kind: that's where the ghost-vigil comes in. Jane, his daughter and heiress (and Sir Lucas was if anything even better off than

Sir Charles) is a pretty little thing of eighteen of whom all you can really say is that she's a pretty little thing of eighteen. Then there's Mörike, the man I've arrested: thin, thirtyish, a Luftwaffe pilot during the war, and at present an architecture student working over here under one of these exchange schemes the Universities are always getting up – which accounts for Sir Charles' knowing him and inviting him to the house party. Last of the important guests – important from the point of view of the crime, that is – is a C.I.D. man (not Metropolitan, Sussex County) called James Wilburn. He's important because the evidence he provides is quite certainly reliable – there has to be a *point d'appui* in these affairs, and Wilburn is it, so you mustn't exhaust yourself doubting his word about anything.'

'I won't,' Fen promised. 'I'll believe him.'

'Good. At dinner on Christmas Eve, then, the conversation turns to the subject of the Rydalls ghost – and I've ascertained that the person responsible for bringing this topic up was Otto Mörike. So far, so good: the Rydalls ghost was a bait Sir Lucas could be relied on to rise to, and rise to it he did, arranging eventually with his rather reluctant host to go down to the pavilion after dinner and keep watch there for an hour or two. The time arriving, he was accompanied to the place of trial by Sir Charles and by Wilburn – neither of whom actually *entered* the pavilion. Wilburn strolled back to the house alone, leaving Sir Charles and Sir Lucas talking shop. And presently Sir Charles, having seen Sir Lucas go into the pavilion, retraced his steps likewise, arriving at the house just in time to hear the alarm-bell ringing.'

'Alarm-bell?'

'People had watched for the ghost before, and there was a bell installed in the pavilion for them to ring if for any reason they wanted help. … This bell sounded, then, at shortly after ten o'clock, and a whole party of people, including Sir Charles, Jane Welsh and Wilburn, hastened to the rescue.

'Now, you must know that this pavilion is quite small. There's just one circular room to it, having two windows (both very firmly nailed up); and you get into this room by way of a longish, narrow hall projecting from the perimeter of the circle, the one and only door being at the outer end of this hall.'

'Like a key-hole,' Fen suggested. 'If you saw it from the air it'd look like a key-hole, I mean; with the round part representing the room, and the part where the wards go in representing the entrance-hall, and the door right down at the bottom.'

'That's it. It stands in a clearing among the trees of the park, on a very slight rise – inferior Palladian in style, with pilasters or whatever you call them: something like a decayed miniature classical temple. No one's bothered about it for decades, not since that earlier murder put an end to its career as a love-nest for a succession of squires. What is it Eliot says? – something about lusts and dead limbs? Well, anyway, that's the impression it gives. A *house* is all right, because a house has been used for other things as well – eating and reading and births and deaths and so on. But this place has been used for one purpose and one purpose only, and that's exactly what it feels like. …

'There's no furniture in it, by the way. And until the wretched Sir Lucas unlocked its door, no one had been inside it for two or three years.

'To get back to the story, then.

'The weather was all right: you'll remember that on Christmas Eve none of this snow and foulness had started. And the rescue-party, so to call them, seem to have regarded their expedition as more or less in the nature of a jaunt; I mean that they weren't seriously alarmed at the ringing of the bell, with the exception of Jane, who knew her father well enough to suspect that he'd never have interrupted his vigil, almost as soon as it had begun, for the sake of a rather futile practical joke; and even she seems to have allowed herself to be half convinced by the reassurances of the others. On arrival at the pavilion, they found the door shut but not locked; and when they opened it, and shone their torches inside, they saw a single set of footprints in the dust on the hall floor, leading to the entrance to the circular room. Acting on instinct or training or both, Wilburn kept his crowd clear of these footprints; and so it was that they came – joined now by Otto Mörike, who according to his subsequent statement had been taking a solitary stroll in the grounds – to the scene of the crime.

'Fireplace, two windows, a crudely painted ceiling – crude in subject as well as in execution – a canvas chair, an unlit electric torch, festoons of cobwebs, and on everything except the chair and the torch *dust*, layers of it. Sir Lucas was lying on the floor beneath one of the windows, quite close to the bell-push; and an old stiletto, later discovered to have been stolen from the house, had been stuck into him under the left shoulder-blade (no damning fingerprints on it, by the way; or on anything else in the vicinity). Sir Lucas was still alive, and just conscious. Wilburn bent over him to ask who was responsible. And a queer smile crossed Sir Lucas' face, and he was just able to whisper' – here Humbleby produced and consulted a notebook – 'to whisper: *"Wrote it – on the window. Very first thing I did when I came round. Did it before I rang the bell or anything else, in case you didn't get here in time – in time for me to tell you who –"*

'His voice faded out then. But with a final effort he

moved his head, glanced up at the window, nodded and smiled again. That was how he died.

'They had all heard him, and they all looked. There was bright moonlight outside, and the letters traced on the grimy pane stood out clearly.

'Otto.

'Well, it seems that then Otto started edging away, and Sir Charles made a grab at him, and they fought, and presently a wallop from Sir Charles sent Otto clean through the tell-tale window, and Sir Charles scrambled after him, and they went on fighting outside, trampling the glass to smithereens, until Wilburn and company joined in and put a stop to it. Incidentally, Wilburn says that Otto's going through the window looked *contrived* to him – a deliberate attempt to destroy evidence; though of course, so many people *saw* the name written there that it remains perfectly good evidence in spite of having been destroyed.'

'Motive ?' Fen asked.

'Good enough. Jane Welsh was wanting to marry Otto – had fallen quite dementedly in love with him, in fact – and her father didn't approve; partly on the grounds that Otto was a German, and partly because he thought the boy wanted Jane's prospective inheritance rather than Jane herself. To clinch it, moreover, there was the fact that Otto had been in the Luftwaffe and that Jane's mother had been killed in 1941 in an air-raid. Jane being only eighteen years of age – and the attitude of magistrates, if appealed to, being in the circumstances at best problematical – it looked as if that was one marriage that would definitely not take place. So the killing of Sir Lucas had, from Otto's point of view, a double advantage: it made Jane rich, and it removed the obstacle to the marriage.'

'Jane's prospective guardian not being against it.'

'Jane's prospective guardian being an uncle she could twist round her little finger.... But here's the point.' Humbleby leaned forward earnestly. 'Here is the point: windows nailed shut; no secret doors – emphatically none; chimney too narrow to admit a baby; and in the dust on the hall floor, only one set of footprints, made unquestionably by Sir Lucas himself.... If you're thinking that Otto might have walked in and out on top of those prints, as that page-boy we've been hearing so much about recently did with King Wenceslaus, then you're wrong. Otto's feet are much too large, for one thing, and the prints hadn't been disturbed, for another: so that's out. But then, how on earth did he manage it? There's no furniture in that hall whatever – nothing he could have used to crawl across, nothing he could have swung himself from. It's a long, bare box, that's all; and the distance between the door and the circular room (in which room, by the way, the dust on the floor was all messed up by the rescue-party) is miles too far for anyone to have jumped it. Nor was the weapon the sort of thing that could possibly have been fired from a bow or an air-gun or a blow-pipe, or any nonsense of that sort; nor was it sharp enough or heavy enough to have penetrated as deeply as it did if it had been *thrown*. So ghosts apart, what *is* the explanation? Can you see one?'

Fen made no immediate reply. Throughout this narrative he had remained standing, draped against the mantelpiece. Now he moved, collecting Humbleby's empty glass and his own and carrying them across to the decanter; and it was only after they were refilled that he spoke.

'Supposing,' he said, 'that Otto had crossed the entrance hall on a tricycle – '

'A tricycle!' Humbleby was dumbfounded. 'A – '

'A tricycle, yes,' Fen reiterated firmly. 'Or supposing, again, that he had laid down a carpet, unrolling it in front of him as he entered and rolling it up again after him when he left....'

'But the dust!' wailed Humbleby. 'Have I really not made it clear to you that apart from the footprints the dust on the floor was undisturbed? Tricycles, carpets....'

'A section of the floor at least,' Fen pointed out, 'was trampled on by the rescue-party.'

'Oh, that. ... Yes, but that didn't happen until after Wilburn had examined the floor.'

'Examined it in detail?'

'Yes. At that stage they still didn't realize anything was

wrong; and when Wilburn led them in they were giggling behind him while he did a sort of parody of detective work, throwing the beam of his torch over every inch of the floor in a pretended search for bloodstains.'

'It doesn't,' said Fen puritanically, 'sound the sort of performance which would amuse me very much.'

'I dare say not. Anyway, the point about it is that Wilburn's ready to swear that the dust was completely unmarked and undisturbed except for the footprints.... I wish he weren't ready to swear that,' Humbleby added dolefully, 'because that's what's holding me up. But I can't budge him.'

'You oughtn't to be trying to budge him, anyway,' retorted Fen, whose mood of self-righteousness appeared to be growing on him. 'It's unethical. What about blood, now?'

'Blood? There was practically none of it. You don't get any bleeding to speak of from that narrow type of wound.'

'Ah. Just one more question, then; and if the answer's what I expect, I shall be able to tell you how Otto worked it.'

'If by any remote chance,' said Humblebly suspiciously, 'it's *stilts* that you have in mind – '

'My dear Humbleby, don't be so puerile.'

Humbleby contained himself with an effort. 'Well?' he said.

'The name on the window.' Fen spoke almost dreamily. 'Was it written in *capital* letters?'

Whatever Humbleby had been expecting, it was clearly not this. 'Yes,' he answered. 'But – '

'Wait.' Fen drained his glass. 'Wait while I make a telephone call.'

He went. All at once restless, Humbleby got to his feet, lit a cheroot, and began pacing the room. Presently he discovered an elastic-driven aeroplane abandoned behind an armchair, wound it up and launched it. It caught Fen a glancing blow on the temple as he reappeared in the doorway, and thence flew on into the hall, where it struck and smashed a vase. 'Oh, I say, I'm sorry,' said Humbleby feebly. Fen said nothing.

But after about half a minute, when he had simmered down a bit: 'Locked rooms,' he remarked sourly. 'Locked rooms – I'll tell you what it is, Humbleby: you've been reading too much fiction; you've got locked rooms on the brain.'

Humbleby thought it politic to be meek. 'Yes,' he said.

'Gideon Fell once gave a very brilliant lecture on The Locked-Room Problem, in connection with that business of the Hollow Man; but there was one category he didn't include.'

'Well?'

Fen massaged his forehead resentfully. 'He didn't include the locked-room mystery which *isn't* a locked-room mystery: like this one. So that the explanation of how Otto got into and out of that circular room is simple: he didn't get into or out of it at all.'

Humbleby gaped. 'But Sir Lucas can't have been knifed before he *entered* the circular room. Sir Charles said – '

'Ah yes. Sir Charles saw him go in – or so he asserts. And – '

'Stop a bit.' Humbleby was much perturbed. 'I can see what you're getting at, but there are serious objections to it.'

'Such as?'

'Well, for one thing, Sir Lucas *named* his murderer.'

'A murderer who struck at him *from behind*…. Oh, I've no doubt Sir Lucas acted in good faith: Otto, you see, would be the only member of the house party whom Sir Lucas *knew* to have a *motive*. In actual fact, Sir Charles had one too – as I've just discovered. But Sir Lucas wasn't aware of that; and in any case, he very particularly didn't want Otto to marry his daughter after his death, so that the risk of doing an ex-Luftwaffe man an injustice was a risk he was prepared to take. Next objection?'

'The name on the window. If, as Sir Lucas said, his *very first* action on recovering consciousness was to denounce his attacker, then he'd surely, since he was capable of entering the pavilion after being knifed, have been capable of writing the name on the *outside* of the window, which would be nearest, and which was just as grimy as the inside. That objection's based, of course, on your assumption that he was struck before he ever entered the pavilion.'

'I expect he did just that – wrote the name on the outside of the window, I mean.'

'But the people who saw it were on the *inside*. Inside a bank, for instance, haven't you ever noticed how the bank's name – '

'The name Otto,' Fen interposed, 'is a palindrome. That's to say, it reads the same backwards as forwards. What's more, the capital letters used in it are symmetrical – not like B or P or R or S, but like A or H or M. So write it on the outside of a window, and it will look exactly the same from the inside.'

'My God, yes.' Humbleby was sobered. 'I never thought of that. And the fact that the name was on the *outside* would be fatal to Sir Charles, after his assertion that he'd seen Sir Lucas enter the pavilion unharmed, so I suppose that the "contriving" Wilburn noticed in the fight was Sir Charles' not Otto's: he'd realize that the name *must* be on the outside – Sir Lucas having said that the writing of it was the very first thing he did – and he'd see the need to destroy the window before anyone could investigate closely. … Wait, though: couldn't Sir Lucas have entered the pavilion as Sir Charles said, and later emerged again, and – '

'One set of footprints,' Fen pointed out, 'on the hall floor. Not three.'

Humbleby nodded. 'I've been a fool about this. Locked rooms, as you said, on the brain. But what *was* Sir Charles' motive – the motive Sir Lucas didn't know about?'

'Belchester,' said Fen. 'Belchester Cathedral. As you know, it was bombed during the war, and a new one's going to be built. Well, I've just rung up the Dean, who's an acquaintance of mine, to ask about the choice of architect; and he says that it was a toss-up between Sir Charles' design and Sir Lucas', and that Sir Lucas' won. The two men were notified by post, and it seems likely that Sir Charles' notification arrived on the morning of Christmas Eve. Sir Lucas' did too, in all probability; but Sir Lucas' was sent to his home, and even forwarded it can't, in the rush of Christmas postal traffic, have reached him at Rydalls before he was killed. So only Sir Charles *knew;* and since with Sir Lucas dead Sir Charles' design would have been accepted. ...' Fen shrugged. 'Was it money, I wonder? Or was it just the blow to his professional pride? Well, well. Let's have another drink before you telephone. In the hangman's shed it will all come to the same thing.'

A Traditional Christmas

Val McDermid

Last night, I dreamed I went to Amberley. Snow had fallen, deep and crisp and even, garlanding the trees like tinsel sparkling in the sunlight as we swept through the tall iron gates and up the drive. Diana was driving, her gloved hands assured on the wheel in spite of the hazards of an imperfectly cleared surface. We rounded the coppice, and there was the house, perfect as a photograph, the sun seeming to breathe life into the golden Cotswold stone. Amberley House, one of the little jobs Vanbrugh knocked off once he'd learned the trade with Blenheim Palace.

Diana stopped in front of the portico and blared the horn. She turned to me, eyes twinkling, smile bewitching as ever. 'Christmas begins here,' she said. As if on cue, the front door opened and Edmund stood framed in the doorway, flanked by his and Diana's mother, and his wife Jane, all smiling as gaily as daytrippers.

I woke then, rigid with shock, pop-eyed in the dark. It was one of those dreams so vivid that when you waken, you can't quite believe it has just happened. But I knew it was a dream. A nightmare, rather. For Edmund, sixth Baron Amberley of Anglezarke had been dead for three months. I should know. I found the body.

Beside me, Diana was still asleep. I wanted to burrow into her side, seeking comfort from the horrors of memory, but I couldn't bring myself to be so selfish. A proper night's sleep was still a luxury for her and the next couple of weeks weren't exactly going to be restful. I slipped out of bed and went through to the kitchen to make a cup of camomile tea.

I huddled over the gas fire and forced myself to think back to Christmas. It was the fourth year that Diana and I had made the trip back to her ancestral home to celebrate. As our first Christmas together had approached, I'd worried about what we were going to do. In relationships like ours, there isn't a standard formula. The only thing I was sure about was that I wanted us to spend it together. I knew that meant visiting my parents was out. As long as they never have to confront the physical evidence of my lesbianism, they can handle it. Bringing any woman home to their tenement flat in Glasgow for Christmas would be uncomfortable. Bringing the daughter of a baron would be impossible.

When I'd nervously broached the subject, Diana had looked astonished, her eyebrows raised, her mouth twitching in a half-smile. 'I assumed you'd want to come to Amberley with me,' she said. 'They're expecting you to.'

'Are you sure?'

Diana grabbed me in a bear-hug. 'Of course I'm sure. Don't you want to spend Christmas with me?'

'Stupid question,' I grunted. 'I thought maybe we could celebrate on our own, just the two of us. Romantic, intimate, that sort of thing.'

Diana looked uncertain. 'Can't we be romantic at Amberley? I can't imagine Christmas anywhere else. It's so … traditional. So English.'

My turn for the raised eyebrows. 'Sure I'll fit in?'

'You know my mother thinks the world of you. She insists on you coming. She's fanatical about tradition, especially Christmas. You'll love it,' she promised.

And I did. Unlikely as it is, this Scottish working-class lesbian feminist homeopath fell head over heels for the whole English country-house package. I loved driving down with Diana on Christmas Eve, leaving the motorway traffic behind, slipping through narrow lanes with their tall hedgerows, driving through the chocolate-box village of Amberley, fairy lights strung round the green, and, finally, cruising past the Dower House where her mother lived and on up the drive. I loved the sherry and mince pies with the neighbours, even the ones who wanted to regale me with their ailments. I loved the elaborate Christmas Eve meal Diana's mother cooked. I loved the brisk walk through the woods to the village church for the midnight service. I loved most of all the way they simply absorbed me into their ritual without distance.

Christmas Day was champagne breakfast, stockings crammed with childish toys and expensive goodies from the Sloane Ranger shops, church again, then presents proper. The gargantuan feast of Christmas dinner, with free-range turkey from the estate's home farm. Then a dozen close family friends arrived to pull crackers, wear silly hats and masks, drink like tomorrow was another life and play every ridiculous party game from sardines to charades. I'm glad no one's ever videotaped the evening and threatened to send a copy to the women's alternative health co-operative where I practise. I'd have to pay the blackmail. Diana and I lead a classless life in London, where almost no one knows her background. It's not that she's embarrassed. It's just that she knows from bitter experience how many barriers it builds for her. But at Amberley, we left behind my homeopathy and her Legal Aid practice, and for a few days we lived in a time warp that Charles Dickens would have revelled in.

On Boxing Day night, we always trooped down to the village hall for the dance. It was then that Edmund came into his own. His huntin', shootin' and fishin' persona slipped from him like the masks we'd worn the night before when he picked up his alto sax and stepped onto the stage to lead the twelve-piece Amber Band. Most of his fellow members were professional session musicians, but the drummer doubled as a labourer on Amberley Farm and the keyboard player was the village postman. I'm no connoisseur, but I reckoned the Amber Band was one of the best live outfits I've ever heard. They played everything from Duke Ellington to Glenn Miller, including Miles Davis and John Coltrane pieces, all arranged by Edmund. And of course, they played some of Edmund's own compositions, strange haunting slow-dancing pieces that somehow achieved the seemingly impossible marriage between the English countryside and jazz.

There was nothing different to mark out last Christmas as a watershed gig. Edmund led the band with his usual verve. Diana and I danced with each other half the night and took it in turns to dance with her mother the rest of the time. Evangeline ('call me Evie') still danced with a vivacity and flair that made me understand why Diana's father had fallen for her. As usual, Jane sat stolidly nursing a gin and tonic that she made last the whole night. 'I don't dance,' she'd said stiffly to me when I'd asked her up on my first visit. It was a rebuff that brooked no argument. Later, I asked Diana if Jane had knocked me back because I was a dyke.

Diana roared with laughter. 'Good God, no,' she spluttered. 'Jane doesn't even dance with Edmund. She's tone deaf and has no sense of rhythm.'

'Bit of a handicap, being married to Edmund,' I said.

Diana shrugged. 'It would be if music were the only thing he did. But the Amber Band only does a few gigs a year. The rest of the time he's running the estate and Jane loves being the country squire's wife.'

In the intervening years, that was the only thing that had changed. Word of mouth had increased the demand for the Amber Band's services. By last Christmas, the band were playing at least one gig a week. They'd moved up from playing village halls and hunt balls onto the student-union circuit.

Last Christmas I'd gone for a walk with Diana's mother on the afternoon of Christmas Eve. As we'd emerged from the back door, I noticed a three-ton van parked over by the stables. Along the side, in tall letters of gold and black, it said, 'Amber Band! Bringing jazz to the people.'

'Wow,' I said. 'That looks serious.'

Evie laughed. 'It keeps Edmund happy. His father was obsessed with breaking the British record for the largest salmon, which, believe me, was a far more inconvenient interest than Edmund's. All Jane has to put up with is a lack of Edmund's company two or three nights a week at most. Going alone to a dinner party is a far lighter cross to bear than being dragged off to fishing lodges in the middle of nowhere to be bitten to death by midges.'

'Doesn't he find it hard, trying to run the estate as well?' I asked idly as we struck out across the park towards the coppice.

Evie's lips pursed momentarily, but her voice betrayed no irritation. 'He's taken a man on part-time to take care of the day-to-day business. Edmund keeps his hands firmly on the reins, but Lewis has taken on the burden of much of the routine work.'

'It can't be easy, making an estate like this pay nowadays.'

Evie smiled. 'Edmund's very good at it. He understands the importance of tradition, but he's not afraid to try new things. I'm very lucky with my children, Jo. They've turned out better than any mother could have hoped.'

I accepted the implied compliment in silence.

The happy family idyll crashed around everyone's ears the day after Boxing Day. Edmund had seemed quieter than usual over lunch, but I put that down to the hangover that, if there were any justice in the world, he should be suffering. As Evie poured out the coffee, he cleared his throat and said abruptly, I've got something to say to you all.'

Diana and I exchanged questioning looks. I noticed Jane's face freeze, her fingers clutching the handle of her coffee cup. Evie finished what she was doing and sat down. 'We're all listening, Edmund,' she said gently.

'As you're all aware, Amber Band has become increasingly successful. A few weeks ago, I was approached by a representative of a major record company. They would like us to sign a deal with them to make some recordings. They would also like to help us move our touring venues up a gear or two. I've discussed this with the band, and we're all agreed that we would be crazy to turn our backs on this opportunity.' Edmund paused and looked around apprehensively.

'Congratulations, bro,' Diana said. I could hear the nervousness in her voice, though I wasn't sure why she was so apprehensive. I sat silent, waiting for the other shoe to drop.

'Go on,' Evie said in a voice so unemotional it sent a chill to my heart.

'Obviously, this is something that has implications for Amberley. I can't have a career as a musician and continue to be responsible for all of this. Also, we need to increase the income from the estate in order to make sure that whatever happens to my career, there will always be enough money available to allow Ma to carry on as she has always done. So I have made the decision to hand over the running of the house and the estate to a management company who will run the house as a residential conference centre and manage the land in broad accordance with the principles I've already established,' Edmund said in a rush.

Jane's face flushed dark red. 'How dare you?' she hissed. 'You can't turn this place into some bloody talking shop. The house will be full of ghastly sales reps. Our lives won't be our own.'

Edmund looked down at the table. 'We won't be here,' he said softly. 'It makes more sense if we move out. I thought we could take a house in London.' He looked up beseechingly at Jane, a look so naked it was embarrassing to witness it.

'This is extraordinary,' Evie said, finding her voice at last. 'Hundreds of years of tradition, and you want to smash it to pieces to indulge some hobby?'

Edmund took a deep breath. 'Ma, it's not a hobby. It's the only time I feel properly alive. Look, this is not a matter for discussion. I've made my mind up. The house and the estate are mine absolutely to do with as I see fit, and these are my plans. There's no point in argument. The papers are all drawn up and I'm going to town tomorrow to sign them. The other chaps from the village have already handed in their notice. We're all set.'

Jane stood up. 'You bastard,' she yelled. 'You inconsiderate bastard! Why didn't you discuss this with me?'

Edmund raised his hands out to her. 'I knew you'd be opposed to it. And you know how hard I find it to say no to you. Jane, I need to do this. It'll be fine, I promise you. We'll find somewhere lovely to live in London, near your friends.'

Wordlessly, Jane picked up her coffee cup and hurled it at Edmund. It caught him in the middle of the forehead. He barely flinched as the hot liquid poured down his face, turning his sweater brown. 'You insensitive pig,' she said in a low voice. 'Hadn't you noticed I haven't had a period for two months? I'm pregnant, Edmund, you utter bastard. I'm two months pregnant and you want to turn my life upside down?' Then she ran from the room slamming the heavy door behind her, no mean feat in itself.

In the stunned silence that followed Jane's bombshell, no one moved. Then Edmund, his face seeming to disintegrate, pushed his chair back with a screech and hurried wordlessly after his wife. I turned to look at Diana. The sight of her stricken face was like a blow to the chest. I barely registered Evie sighing, 'How sharper than a serpent's tooth,' before she too left the room. Before the door closed behind her, I was out of my chair, Diana pressed close to me.

Dinner that evening was the first meal I'd eaten at Amberley in an atmosphere of strain. Hardly a word was spoken, and I suspect I wasn't alone in feeling relief when

Edmund rose abruptly before coffee and announced he was going down to the village to rehearse. 'Don't wait up,' he said tersely.

Jane went upstairs as soon as the meal was over. Evie sat down with us to watch a film, but half an hour into it, she rose and said, 'I'm sorry. I'm not concentrating. Your brother has given me rather too much to think about. I'm going back to the Dower House.'

Diana and I walked to the door with her mother. We stood under the portico, watching the dark figure against the snow. The air was heavy, the sky lowering. 'Feels like a storm brewing,' Diana remarked. 'Even the weather's cross with Edmund.'

We watched the rest of the film then decided to go up to bed. As we walked through the hall, I went to switch off the lights on the Christmas tree. 'Leave them,' Diana said. 'Edmund will turn them off when he comes in. It's tradition – last to bed does the tree.' She smiled reminiscently. 'The number of times I've come back from parties in the early hours and seen the tree shining down the drive.'

About an hour later, the storm broke. We were reading in bed when a clap of thunder as loud as a bomb blast crashed over the house. Then a rattle of machine-gun fire against the window. We clutched each other in surprise, though heaven knows we've never needed an excuse. Diana slipped out of bed and pulled back one of the heavy damask curtains so we could watch the hail pelt the window and the bolts of lightning flash jagged across the sky. It raged for nearly half an hour. Diana and I played the game of counting the gap between thunderclaps and lightning flashes, which told us the storm seemed to be circling Amberley itself, moving off only to come back and blast us again with lightning and hail.

Eventually it moved off to the west, occasional flashes lighting up the distant hills. Somehow, it seemed the right time to make love. As we lay together afterwards, revelling in the luxury of satiated sensuality, the lights suddenly went out. 'Damn,' Diana drawled. 'Bloody storm's got the electrics on the blink.' She stirred. 'I'd better go down and check the fuse box.'

I grabbed her. 'Leave it,' I urged. 'Edmund can do it when he comes in. We're all warm and sleepy. Besides, I might get lonely.'

Diana chuckled and snuggled back into my arms. Moments later, the lights came back on again. 'See?' I said. 'No need. Probably a problem at the local sub-station because of the weather.'

I woke up just after seven the following morning, full of the joys of spring. We were due to go back to London after lunch, so I decided to sneak out for an early morning walk in the copse. I dressed without waking Diana and slipped out of the silent house.

The path from the house to the copse was well-trodden. There had been no fresh snow since Christmas Eve, and the path was well used, since it was a short cut both to the Dower House and the village. There were even mountain-bike tracks among the scattered boot prints. The trees, an elderly mixture of beech, birch, alder, oak and ash, still held their tracery of snow on the tops of some branches, though following the storm a mild thaw had set in. As I moved into the wood, I felt drips of melting snow on my head.

In the middle of the copse, there's a clearing fringed with silver birch trees. When she was little, Diana was convinced this was the place where the fairies came to recharge their magic. There was no magic in the clearing that morning. As soon as I emerged from the trees, I saw Edmund's body, sprawled under a single silver birch tree by the path on the far side.

For a moment, I was frozen with shock. Then I rushed forward and crouched down beside him. I didn't need to feel for a pulse. He was clearly long dead, his right hand blackened and burned.

I can't remember the next hours. Apparently, I went to the Dower House and roused Evie. I blurted out what I'd seen and she called the police. I have a vague recollection of her staggering slightly as I broke the news, but I was in shock and I have no recollection of what she said. Diana arrived soon afterwards. When her mother told her what had happened, she stared numbly at me for a moment, then tears poured down her face. None of us seemed eager to be the one to break the news to Jane. Eventually, as if by mutual consent, we waited until the police arrived. We merited two uniformed constables, plus two plain-clothes detectives. In the words of Noel Coward, Detective Inspector Maggie Staniforth would not have fooled a drunken child of two and a half. As soon as Evie introduced me as her daughter's partner, DI Staniforth thawed visibly. I didn't much care at that point. I was too numbed even to take in what they were saying. It sounded like the distant mutter of bees in a herb garden.

DI Staniforth set off with her team to examine the body while Diana and I, after a muttered discussion in the corner, informed Evie that we would go and tell Jane. We found her in the kitchen drinking a mug of coffee. 'I don't suppose you've seen my husband,' she said in tones of utter contempt when we walked in. 'He didn't have the courage to come home last night.'

Diana sat down next to Jane and flashed me a look of panic. I stepped forward. 'I'm sorry, Jane, but there's been an accident.' In moments of crisis, why is it we always reach for the nearest cliché?

Jane looked at me as if I were speaking Swahili. 'An accident?' she asked in a macabre echo of Dame Edith Evans's 'A handbag?'

'Edmund's dead,' Diana blurted out. 'He was struck by lightning in the wood. Coming home from the village.'

As she spoke, a wave of nausea surged through me. I thought I was going to faint. I grabbed the edge of the table. Diana's words robbed the muscles in my legs of their strength and I lurched into the nearest chair. Up until that point, I'd been too dazed with shock to realise the conclusion everyone but me had come to.

Jane looked blankly at Diana. 'I'm so sorry,' Diana said, the tears starting again, flowing down her cheeks.

'I'm not,' Jane said. 'He can't stop my child growing up in Amberley now.'

Diana turned white. 'You bitch,' she said wonderingly.

At least I knew then what I had to do.

Maggie Staniforth arrived shortly after to interview me. 'It's just a formality,' she said. 'It's obvious what happened. He was walking home in the storm and was struck by lightning as he passed under the birch tree.'

I took a deep breath. 'I'm afraid not,' I said. 'Edmund was murdered.'

Her eyebrows rose. 'You're still in shock. I'm afraid there are no suspicious circumstances.'

'Maybe not to you. But I know different.'

Credit where it's due, she heard me out. But the sceptical look never left her eyes. 'That's all very well,' she said eventually. 'But if what you're saying is true, there's no way of proving it.'

I shrugged. 'Why don't you look for fingerprints? Either in the plug of the Christmas tree lights, or on the main fuse box. When he was electrocuted, the lights fused. At the time, Diana and I thought it was a glitch in the mains supply, but we know better now. Jane would have had to rewire the plug and the socket to cover her tracks. And she must have gone down to the cellar to repair the fuse or turn the circuit breaker back on. She wouldn't have had occasion to touch those in the usual run of things. I doubt she'd even have good reason to know where the fuse box is. Try it,' I urged.

And that's how Evie came to be charged with the murder of her son. If I'd thought things through, if I'd waited till my brain was out of shock, I'd have realised that Jane would never have risked her baby by hauling Edmund's body over the crossbar of his mountain bike and wheeling him out to the copse. Besides, she probably believed she could use his love for her to persuade him to change his mind. Evie didn't have that hope to cling to.

If I'd realised it was Diana's mother who killed Edmund, I doubt very much if I'd have shared my esoteric knowledge with DI Staniforth. It's a funny business, New Age medicine. When I attended a seminar on the healing powers of plants given by a Native American medicine man, I never thought his wisdom would help me prove a murder.

Maybe Evie will get lucky. Maybe she'll get a jury reluctant to convict in a case that rests on the inexplicable fact that lightning never strikes birch trees.

The Adventure of the Blue Carbuncle

Arthur Conan Doyle

I had called upon my friend Sherlock Holmes upon the second morning after Christmas, with the intention of wishing him the compliments of the season. He was lounging upon the sofa in a purple dressing-gown, a pipe-rack within his reach upon the right, and a pile of crumpled morning papers, evidently newly studied, near at hand. Beside the couch was a wooden chair, and on the angle of the back hung a very seedy and disreputable hard-felt hat, much the worse for wear, and cracked in several places. A lens and a forceps lying upon the seat of the chair suggested that the hat had been suspended in this manner for the purpose of examination.

'You are engaged,' said I; 'perhaps I interrupt you.'

'Not at all. I am glad to have a friend with whom I can discuss my results. The matter is a perfectly trivial one' (he jerked his thumb in the direction of the old hat) 'but there are points in connection with it which are not entirely devoid of interest and even of instruction.'

I seated myself in his armchair and warmed my hands before his crackling fire, for a sharp frost had set in, and the windows were thick with the ice crystals. 'I suppose,' I remarked, 'that, homely as it looks, this thing has some deadly story linked on to it – that it is the clue which will guide you in the solution of some mystery and the punishment of some crime.'

'No, no. No crime,' said Sherlock Holmes, laughing. 'Only one of those whimsical little incidents which will happen when you have four million human beings all jostling each other within the space of a few square miles. Amid the action and reaction of so dense a swarm of humanity, every possible combination of events may be expected to take place, and many a little problem will be presented which may be striking and bizarre without being criminal. We have already had experience of such.'

'So much so,' I remarked, 'that of the last six cases which I have added to my notes, three have been entirely free of any legal crime.'

'Precisely. You allude to my attempt to recover the Irene

Adler papers, to the singular case of Miss Mary Suther-
land, and to the adventure of the man with the twisted
lip. Well, I have no doubt that this small matter will fall
into the same innocent category. You know Peterson, the
commissionaire?'

'Yes.'

'It is to him that this trophy belongs.'

'It is his hat.'

'No, no, he found it. Its owner is unknown. I beg that
you will look upon it not as a battered billycock but as an
intellectual problem. And, first, as to how it came here.
It arrived upon Christmas morning, in company with a
good fat goose, which is, I have no doubt, roasting at this
moment in front of Peterson's fire. The facts are these:
about four o'clock on Christmas morning, Peterson,
who, as you know, is a very honest fellow, was returning from some small jollification and was making his way
homeward down Tottenham Court Road. In front of
him he saw, in the gaslight, a tallish man, walking with a
slight stagger, and carrying a white goose slung over his
shoulder. As he reached the corner of Goodge Street, a
row broke out between this stranger and a little knot of
roughs. One of the latter knocked off the man's hat, on
which he raised his stick to defend himself and, swinging
it over his head, smashed the shop window behind him.
Peterson had rushed forward to protect the stranger from

his assailants; but the man, shocked at having broken the window, and seeing an official-looking person in uniform rushing towards him, dropped his goose, took to his heels, and vanished amid the labyrinth of small streets which lie at the back of Tottenham Court Road. The roughs had also fled at the appearance of Peterson, so that he was left in possession of the field of battle, and also of the spoils of victory in the shape of this battered hat and a most unimpeachable Christmas goose.'

'Which surely he restored to their owner?'

'My dear fellow, there lies the problem. It is true that 'For Mrs Henry Baker' was printed upon a small card which was tied to the bird's left leg, and it is also true that the initials 'H.B.' are legible upon the lining of this hat, but as there are some thousands of Bakers, and some hundreds of Henry Bakers in this city of ours, it is not easy to restore lost property to any one of them.'

'What, then, did Peterson do?'

'He brought round both hat and goose to me on Christmas morning, knowing that even the smallest problems are of interest to me. The goose we retained until this morning, when there were signs that, in spite of the slight frost, it would be well that it should be eaten without unnecessary delay. Its finder has carried it off, therefore, to fulfil the ultimate destiny of a goose, while I continue to retain the hat of the gentleman who lost his Christmas dinner.'

'Did he not advertise?'

'No.'

'Then, what clue could you have as to his identity?'

'Only as much as we can deduce.'

'From his hat?'

'Precisely.'

'But you are joking. What can you gather from this old battered felt?'

'Here is my lens. You know my methods. What can you gather yourself as to the individuality of the man who has worn this article?'

I took the tattered object in my hands and turned it over rather ruefully. It was a very ordinary black hat of the usual round shape, hard and much the worse for wear. The lining had been of red silk, but was a good deal discoloured. There was no maker's name; but, as Holmes had remarked, the initials 'H.B.' were scrawled upon one side. It was pierced in the brim for a hat-securer, but the elastic was missing. For the rest, it was cracked, exceedingly dusty, and spotted in several places, although there seemed to have been some attempt to hide the discoloured patches by smearing them with ink.

'I can see nothing,' said I, handing it back to my friend.

'On the contrary, Watson, you can see everything. You fail, however, to reason from what you see. You are too timid in drawing your inferences.'

'Then, pray tell me what it is that you can infer from this hat?'

He picked it up and gazed at it in the peculiar introspective fashion which was characteristic of him. 'It is perhaps less suggestive than it might have been,' he remarked, 'and yet there are a few inferences which are very distinct, and a few others which represent at least a strong balance of probability. That the man was highly intellectual is of course obvious upon the face of it, and also that he was fairly well-to-do within the last three years, although he has now fallen upon evil days. He had foresight, but has less now than formerly, pointing to a moral retrogression, which, when taken with the decline of his fortunes, seems to indicate some evil influence, probably drink, at work upon him. This may account also for the obvious fact that his wife has ceased to love him.'

'My dear Holmes!'

'He has, however, retained some degree of self-respect,' he continued, disregarding my remonstrance. 'He is a man who leads a sedentary life, goes out little, is out of training entirely, is middle-aged, has grizzled hair which he has had cut within the last few days, and which he anoints with lime-cream. These are the more patent facts which are to be deduced from his hat. Also, by the way, that it is extremely improbable that he has gas laid on in his house.'

'You are certainly joking, Holmes.'

'Not in the least is it possible that even now, when I give you these results, you are unable to see how they are attained?'

'I have no doubt that I am very stupid, but I must confess that I am unable to follow you. For example, how did you deduce that this man was intellectual?'

For answer Holmes clapped the hat upon his head. It came right over the forehead and settled upon the bridge of his nose. 'It is a question of cubic capacity,' said he; 'a man with so large a brain must have something in it.'

'The decline of his fortunes, then?'

'This hat is three years old. These flat brims curled at the edge came in then. It is a hat of the very best quality. Look at the band of ribbed silk and the excellent lining. If this man could afford to buy so expensive a hat three years ago, and has had no hat since, then he has assuredly gone down in the world.'

'Well, that is clear enough, certainly. But how about the foresight and the moral retrogression?'

Sherlock Holmes laughed. 'Here is the foresight,' said he putting his finger upon the little disc and loop of the hat-securer. 'They are never sold upon hats. If this man ordered one, it is a sign of a certain amount of foresight, since he went out of his way to take this precaution against the wind. But since we see that he has broken the elastic and has not troubled to replace it, it is obvious that he has less foresight now than formerly, which is a distinct proof of a weakening nature. On the other hand, he has endeavoured to conceal some of these stains upon the felt by daubing them with ink, which is a sign that he has not entirely lost his self-respect.'

'Your reasoning is certainly plausible.'

'The further points, that he is middle-aged, that his hair is grizzled, that it has been recently cut, and that he uses lime-cream, are all to be gathered from a close examination of the lower part of the lining. The lens discloses a large number of hair-ends, clean cut by the scissors of the barber. They all appear to be adhesive, and there is a distinct odour of lime-cream. This dust, you will observe, is not the gritty, grey dust of the street but the fluffy brown dust of the house, showing that it has been hung up indoors most of the time, while the marks of moisture upon the inside are proof positive that the wearer perspired very freely, and could therefore, hardly be in the best of training.'

'But his wife – you said that she had ceased to love him.'

'This hat has not been brushed for weeks. When I see you, my dear Watson, with a week's accumulation of dust upon your hat, and when your wife allows you to go out in such a state, I shall fear that you also have been unfortunate enough to lose your wife's affection.'

'But he might be a bachelor.'

'Nay, he was bringing home the goose as a peace-offering to his wife. Remember the card upon the bird's leg.'

'You have an answer to everything. But how on earth do you deduce that the gas is not laid on in his house?'

'One tallow stain, or even two, might come by chance; but when I see no less than five, I think that there can be little doubt that the individual must be brought into frequent contact with burning tallow – walks upstairs at night probably with his hat in one hand and a guttering candle in the other. Anyhow, he never got tallow-stains from a gas-jet. Are you satisfied?'

'Well, it is very ingenious,' said I, laughing; 'but since, as you said just now, there has been no crime committed, and no harm done save the loss of a goose, all this seems to be rather a waste of energy.'

Sherlock Holmes had opened his mouth to reply, when the door flew open, and Peterson, the commissionaire, rushed into the apartment with flushed cheeks and the face of a man who is dazed with astonishment.

'The goose, Mr Holmes! The goose, sir!' he gasped.

'Eh? What of it, then? Has it returned to life and flapped off through the kitchen window?' Holmes twisted himself round upon the sofa to get a fairer view of the man's excited face.

'See here, sir! See what my wife found in its crop!' He

held out his hand and displayed upon the centre of the palm a brilliantly scintillating blue stone, rather smaller than a bean in size, but of such purity and radiance that it twinkled like an electric point in the dark hollow of his hand.

Sherlock Holmes sat up with a whistle. 'By Jove, Peterson!' said he, 'this is a treasure trove indeed. I suppose you know what you have got?'

'A diamond, sir? A precious stone. It cuts into glass as though it were putty.'

'It's more than a precious stone. It is *the* precious stone.'

'Not the Countess of Morcar's blue carbuncle!' I ejaculated.

'Precisely so. I ought to know its size and shape, seeing that I have read the advertisement about it in *The Times* every day lately. It is absolutely unique, and its value can only be conjectured, but the reward offered of a thousand pounds is certainly not within a twentieth part of the market price.'

'A thousand pounds! Great Lord of mercy!' The commissionaire plumped down into a chair and stared from one to the other of us.

'That is the reward, and I have reason to know that there are sentimental considerations in the background which would induce the Countess to part with half her fortune if she could but recover the gem.'

'It was lost, if I remember aright, at the Hotel Cosmopolitan,' I remarked.

'Precisely so, on the twenty-second of December, just five days ago. John Horner, a plumber, was accused of having abstracted it from the lady's jewel-case. The evidence against him was so strong that the case has been referred to the Assizes. I have some account of the matter here, I believe.' He rummaged amid his newspapers, glancing over the dates, until at last he smoothed one out, doubled it over, and read the following paragraph:

'Hotel Cosmopolitan Jewel Robbery. John Horner, 26, plumber, was brought up upon the charge of having upon the 22nd inst, abstracted from the jewel-case of the Countess of Morcar the valuable gem known as the blue carbuncle. James Ryder, upper-attendant at the hotel, gave his evidence to the effect that he had shown Horner up to the dressing-room of the Countess of Morcar upon the day of the robbery in order that he might solder the second bar of the grate, which was loose. He had remained with Horner some little time, but had finally been called away. On returning, he found that Horner had disappeared, that the bureau had been forced open, and that the small morocco casket in which, as it afterwards transpired, the Countess was accustomed to keep her jewel, was lying empty upon the dressing-table. Ryder instantly gave the alarm, and Horner was arrested the same evening; but the stone could not be found either upon his person or in his rooms. Catherine Cusack, maid to the Countess, deposed to having heard Ryder's cry of dismay on discovering the robbery, and to having rushed into the room, where she found matters as described by the last witness. Inspector Bradstreet, B division, gave evidence as to the arrest of Horner, who struggled frantically, and protested his innocence in the strongest terms. Evidence of a previous conviction for robbery having been given against the prisoner, the magistrate refused to deal summarily with the offence, but referred it to the Assizes. Horner, who had shown signs of intense emotion during the proceedings, fainted away at the conclusion and was carried out of court.'

'Hum! So much for the police-court,' said Holmes thoughtfully, tossing aside the paper. 'The question for us now to solve is the sequence of events leading from a rifled jewel-case at one end to the crop of a goose in Tottenham Court Road at the other. You see, Watson, our little deductions have suddenly assumed a much more important and less innocent aspect. Here is the stone; the stone came from the goose, and the goose came from Mr Henry Baker, the gentleman with the bad hat and all the other characteristics with which I have bored you. So now we must set ourselves very seriously to finding this gentleman and ascertaining what part he has played in this little mystery. To do this, we must try the simplest means first, and these lie undoubtedly in an advertisement in all the evening papers. If this fail, I shall have recourse to other methods.'

'What will you say?'

'Give me a pencil and that slip of paper. Now, then: "Found at the corner of Goodge Street, a goose and a black felt hat. Mr Henry Baker can have the same by applying at 6:30 this evening at 221B, Baker Street." That is clear and concise.'

'Very. But will he see it?'

'Well, he is sure to keep an eye on the papers, since, to a poor man, the loss was a heavy one. He was clearly so scared by his mischance in breaking the window and by the approach of Peterson that he thought of nothing but flight, but since then he must have bitterly regretted the impulse which caused him to drop his bird. Then, again, the introduction of his name will cause him to see it, for everyone who knows him will direct his attention to it. Here you are, Peterson, run down to the advertising agency and have this put in the evening papers.'

'In which, sir?'

'Oh, in the *Globe*, *Star*, *Pall Mall*, *St James's Gazette*, *Evening News*, *Standard*, *Echo*, and any others that occur to you.'

'Very well, sir. And this stone?'

'Ah, yes, I shall keep the stone. Thank you. And, I say, Peterson, just buy a goose on your way back and leave it here with me, for we must have one to give to this gentleman in place of the one which your family is now devouring.'

When the commissionaire had gone, Holmes took up the stone and held it against the light. 'It's a bonny thing,' said he. 'Just see how it glints and sparkles. Of course it is a nucleus and focus of crime. Every good stone is. They are the devil's pet baits. In the larger and older jewels every facet may stand for a bloody deed. This stone is not yet twenty years old. It was found in the banks of the Amoy River in southern China and is remarkable in having every characteristic of the carbuncle, save that it is blue in shade instead of ruby red. In spite of its youth, it has already a sinister history. There have been two murders, a vitriol-throwing, a suicide, and several robberies brought about for the sake of this forty-grain weight of crystallised charcoal. Who would think that so pretty a toy would be a purveyor to the gallows and the prison? I'll lock it up in my strong box now and drop a line to the Countess to say that we have it.'

'Do you think that this man Horner is innocent?'

'I cannot tell.'

'Well, then, do you imagine that this other one, Henry

Baker, had anything to do with the matter?'

'It is, I think, much more likely that Henry Baker is an absolutely innocent man, who had no idea that the bird which he was carrying was of considerably more value than if it were made of solid gold. That, however, I shall determine by a very simple test if we have an answer to our advertisement.'

'And you can do nothing until then?'

'Nothing.'

'In that case I shall continue my professional round. But I shall come back in the evening at the hour you have mentioned, for I should like to see the solution of so tangled a business.'

'Very glad to see you. I dine at seven. There is a woodcock, I believe. By the way, in view of recent occurrences, perhaps I ought to ask Mrs Hudson to examine its crop.'

I had been delayed at a case, and it was a little after half-past six when I found myself in Baker Street once more. As I approached the house I saw a tall man in a Scotch bonnet with a coat which was buttoned up to his chin waiting outside in the bright semicircle which was thrown from the fanlight. Just as I arrived the door was opened, and we were shown up together to Holmes' room.

'Mr Henry Baker, I believe,' said he, rising from his armchair and greeting his visitor with the easy air of geniality which he could so readily assume. 'Pray take this chair by the fire, Mr Baker. It is a cold night, and I observe that your circulation is more adapted for summer than for winter. Ah, Watson, you have just come at the right time. Is that your hat, Mr Baker?'

'Yes, sir, that is undoubtedly my hat.'

He was a large man with rounded shoulders, a massive head, and a broad, intelligent face, sloping down to a pointed beard of grizzled brown. A touch of red in nose and cheeks, with a slight tremor of his extended hand, recalled Holmes' surmise as to his habits. His rusty black frock-coat was buttoned right up in front, with the collar turned up, and his lank wrists protruded from his sleeves without a sign of cuff or shirt. He spoke in a slow staccato fashion, choosing his words with care, and gave the impression generally of a man of learning and letters who had had ill-usage at the hands of fortune.

'We have retained these things for some days,' said Holmes, 'because we expected to see an advertisement from you giving your address. I am at a loss to know now why you did not advertise.'

Our visitor gave a rather shamefaced laugh. 'Shillings have not been so plentiful with me as they once were,' he remarked. 'I had no doubt that the gang of roughs who assaulted me had carried off both my hat and the bird. I did not care to spend more money in a hopeless attempt at recovering them.'

'Very naturally. By the way, about the bird, we were compelled to eat it.'

'To eat it!' Our visitor half rose from his chair in his excitement.

'Yes, it would have been of no use to anyone had we not done so. But I presume that this other goose upon the sideboard, which is about the same weight and perfectly fresh, will answer your purpose equally well?'

'Oh, certainly, certainly,' answered Mr Baker with a sigh of relief.

'Of course, we still have the feathers, legs, crop, and so on of your own bird, so if you wish – '

The man burst into a hearty laugh. 'They might be useful to me as relics of my adventure,' said he, 'but beyond that I can hardly see what use the *disjecta membra* of my late acquaintance are going to be to me. No, sir, I think that, with your permission, I will confine my attentions to the excellent bird which I perceive upon the sideboard.'

Sherlock Holmes glanced sharply across at me with a slight shrug of his shoulders.

'There is your hat, then, and there your bird,' said he. 'By the way, would it bore you to tell me where you got the other one from? I am somewhat of a fowl fancier, and I have seldom seen a better grown goose.'

'Certainly, sir,' said Baker, who had risen and tucked his newly gained property under his arm. 'There are a few of us who frequent the Alpha Inn, near the Museum – we are to be found in the Museum itself during the day, you understand. This year our good host, Windigate by name, instituted a goose club, by which, on consideration of some few pence every week, we were each to receive a bird at Christmas. My pence were duly paid, and the rest is familiar to you. I am much indebted to you, sir, for a Scotch bonnet is fitted neither to my years nor my gravity.' With a comical pomposity of manner he bowed solemnly to both of us and strode off upon his way.

'So much for Mr Henry Baker,' said Holmes when he had closed the door behind him. 'It is quite certain that he knows nothing whatever about the matter. Are you hungry, Watson?'

'Not particularly.'

'Then I suggest that we turn our dinner into a supper and follow up this clue while it is still hot.'

'By all means.'

It was a bitter night, so we drew on our ulsters and wrapped cravats about our throats. Outside, the stars were shining coldly in a cloudless sky, and the breath of the passers-by blew out into smoke like so many pistol shots. Our footfalls rang out crisply and loudly as we swung through the doctors' quarter, Wimpole Street, Harley Street, and so through Wigmore Street into Oxford Street. In a quarter of an hour we were in Bloomsbury at the Alpha Inn, which is a small public-house at the corner of one of the streets which runs down into Holborn. Holmes pushed open the door of the private bar and ordered two glasses of beer from the ruddy-faced, white-aproned landlord.

'Your beer should be excellent if it is as good as your geese,' said he.

'My geese!' The man seemed surprised.

'Yes. I was speaking only half an hour ago to Mr Henry Baker, who was a member of your goose club.'

'Ah! yes, I see. But you see, sir, them's not our geese.'

'Indeed! Whose, then?'

'Well, I got the two dozen from a salesman in Covent Garden.'

'Indeed? I know some of them. Which was it?'

'Breckinridge is his name.'

'Ah! I don't know him. Well, here's your good health landlord, and prosperity to your house. Good-night.'

'Now for Mr Breckinridge,' he continued, buttoning up his coat as we came out into the frosty air. 'Remember, Watson that though we have so homely a thing as a goose at one end of this chain, we have at the other a man who will certainly get seven years' penal servitude unless we can establish his innocence. It is possible that our inquiry may but confirm his guilt; but, in any case, we have a line of investigation which has been missed by the police, and which a singular chance has placed in our hands. Let us follow it out to the bitter end. Faces to the south, then, and quick march!'

We passed across Holborn, down Endell Street, and so through a zigzag of slums to Covent Garden Market. One of the largest stalls bore the name of Breckinridge upon it, and the proprietor a horsey-looking man, with a sharp face and trim side-whiskers was helping a boy to put up the shutters.

'Good-evening. It's a cold night,' said Holmes.

The salesman nodded and shot a questioning glance at my companion.

'Sold out of geese, I see,' continued Holmes, pointing at the bare slabs of marble.

'Let you have five hundred to-morrow morning.'

'That's no good.'

'Well, there are some on the stall with the gas-flare.'

'Ah, but I was recommended to you.'

'Who by?'

'The landlord of the Alpha.'

'Oh, yes; I sent him a couple of dozen.'

'Fine birds they were, too. Now where did you get them from?'

To my surprise the question provoked a burst of anger from the salesman.

'Now, then, mister,' said he, with his head cocked and

his arms akimbo, 'what are you driving at? Let's have it straight, now.'

'It is straight enough. I should like to know who sold you the geese which you supplied to the Alpha.'

'Well then, I shan't tell you. So now!'

'Oh, it is a matter of no importance; but I don't know why you should be so warm over such a trifle.'

'Warm! You'd be as warm, maybe, if you were as pestered as I am. When I pay good money for a good article there should be an end of the business; but it's "Where are the geese?" and "Who did you sell the geese to?" and "What will you take for the geese?" One would think they were the only geese in the world, to hear the fuss that is made over them.'

'Well, I have no connection with any other people who have been making inquiries,' said Holmes carelessly. 'If you won't tell us the bet is off, that is all. But I'm always ready to back my opinion on a matter of fowls, and I have a fiver on it that the bird I ate is country bred.'

'Well, then, you've lost your fiver, for it's town bred,' snapped the salesman.

'It's nothing of the kind.'

'I say it is.'

'I don't believe it.'

'D'you think you know more about fowls than I, who have handled them ever since I was a nipper? I tell you, all those birds that went to the Alpha were town bred.'

'You'll never persuade me to believe that.'

'Will you bet, then?'

'It's merely taking your money, for I know that I am right. But I'll have a sovereign on with you, just to teach you not to be obstinate.'

The salesman chuckled grimly. 'Bring me the books, Bill,' said he.

The small boy brought round a small thin volume and a great greasy-backed one, laying them out together beneath the hanging lamp.

'Now then, Mr Cocksure,' said the salesman, 'I thought that I was out of geese, but before I finish you'll find that there is still one left in my shop. You see this little book?'

'Well?'

'That's the list of the folk from whom I buy. D'you see? Well, then, here on this page are the country folk, and the numbers after their names are where their accounts are in the big ledger. Now, then! You see this other page in red ink? Well, that is a list of my town suppliers. Now, look at that third name. Just read it out to me.'

'"Mrs Oakshott, 117, Brixton Road – 249",' read Holmes.

'Quite so. Now turn that up in the ledger.'

Holmes turned to the page indicated. 'Here you are, "Mrs. Oakshott, 117, Brixton Road, egg and poultry supplier".'

'Now, then, what's the last entry?'

' "December 22nd. Twenty-four geese at 7s. 6d".'

'Quite so. There you are. And underneath?'

' "Sold to Mr Windigate of the Alpha, at 12s".'

'What have you to say now?'

Sherlock Holmes looked deeply chagrined. He drew a sovereign from his pocket and threw it down upon the slab, turning away with the air of a man whose disgust is too deep for words. A few yards off he stopped under a lamp-post and laughed in the hearty, noiseless fashion which was peculiar to him.

'When you see a man with whiskers of that cut and the "Pink 'un" protruding out of his pocket, you can always draw him by a bet,' said he. 'I daresay that if I had put 100 pounds down in front of him, that man would not have given me such complete information as was drawn from him by the idea that he was doing me on a wager. Well, Watson, we are, I fancy, nearing the end of our quest, and the only point which remains to be determined is whether we should go on to this Mrs Oakshott to-night, or whether we should reserve it for to-morrow. It is clear from what that surly fellow said that there are others besides ourselves who are anxious about the matter, and I should – '

His remarks were suddenly cut short by a loud hubbub which broke out from the stall which we had just left. Turning round we saw a little rat-faced fellow standing in the centre of the circle of yellow light which was thrown by the swinging lamp, while Breckinridge, the salesman, framed in the door of his stall, was shaking his fists fiercely at the cringing figure.

'I've had enough of you and your geese,' he shouted. 'I wish you were all at the devil together. If you come pestering me any more with your silly talk I'll set the dog at you. You bring Mrs Oakshott here and I'll answer her, but what have you to do with it? Did I buy the geese off you?'

'No; but one of them was mine all the same,' whined the little man.

'Well, then, ask Mrs Oakshott for it.'

'She told me to ask you.'

'Well, you can ask the King of Proosia, for all I care. I've had enough of it. Get out of this!' He rushed fiercely forward, and the inquirer flitted away into the darkness.

'Ha! this may save us a visit to Brixton Road,' whispered Holmes. 'Come with me, and we will see what is to be made of this fellow.' Striding through the scattered knots of people who lounged round the flaring stalls, my companion speedily overtook the little man and touched him upon the shoulder. He sprang round, and I could see in the gas-light that every vestige of colour had been driven from his face.

'Who are you, then? What do you want?' he asked in a quavering voice.

'You will excuse me,' said Holmes blandly, 'but I could not help overhearing the questions which you put to the salesman just now. I think that I could be of assistance to you.'

'You? Who are you? How could you know anything of the matter?'

'My name is Sherlock Holmes. It is my business to know what other people don't know.'

'But you can know nothing of this?'

'Excuse me, I know everything of it. You are endeavouring to trace some geese which were sold by Mrs Oakshott, of Brixton Road, to a salesman named Breckinridge, by him in turn to Mr Windigate, of the Alpha, and by him to his club, of which Mr Henry Baker is a member.'

'Oh, sir, you are the very man whom I have longed to meet,' cried the little fellow with outstretched hands and quivering fingers. 'I can hardly explain to you how interested I am in this matter.'

Sherlock Holmes hailed a four-wheeler which was passing. 'In that case we had better discuss it in a cosy room rather than in this wind-swept market-place,' said he. 'But pray tell me, before we go farther, who it is that I have the pleasure of assisting.'

The man hesitated for an instant. 'My name is John Robinson,' he answered with a sidelong glance.

'No, no; the real name,' said Holmes sweetly. 'It is always awkward doing business with an alias.'

A flush sprang to the white cheeks of the stranger. 'Well then,' said he, 'my real name is James Ryder.'

'Precisely so. Head attendant at the Hotel Cosmopolitan. Pray step into the cab, and I shall soon be able to tell you everything which you would wish to know.'

The little man stood glancing from one to the other of us with half-frightened, half-hopeful eyes, as one who is not sure whether he is on the verge of a windfall or of a catastrophe. Then he stepped into the cab, and in half an hour we were back in the sitting-room at Baker Street. Nothing had been said during our drive, but the high, thin breathing of our new companion, and the claspings and unclaspings of his hands, spoke of the nervous tension within him.

'Here we are!' said Holmes cheerily as we filed into the room. 'The fire looks very seasonable in this weather. You look cold, Mr Ryder. Pray take the basket-chair. I will just put on my slippers before we settle this little matter of yours. Now, then! You want to know what became of those geese?'

'Yes, sir.'

'Or rather, I fancy, of that goose. It was one bird, I imagine in which you were interested – white, with a black bar across the tail.'

Ryder quivered with emotion. 'Oh, sir,' he cried, 'can you tell me where it went to?'

'It came here.'

'Here?'

'Yes, and a most remarkable bird it proved. I don't wonder that you should take an interest in it. It laid an egg after it was dead – the bonniest, brightest little blue egg that ever was seen. I have it here in my museum.'

Our visitor staggered to his feet and clutched the mantelpiece with his right hand. Holmes unlocked his strong-box and held up the blue carbuncle, which shone out like a star, with a cold, brilliant, many-pointed radiance. Ryder stood glaring with a drawn face, uncertain whether to claim or to disown it.

'The game's up, Ryder,' said Holmes quietly. 'Hold up, man, or you'll be into the fire! Give him an arm back into his chair, Watson. He's not got blood enough to go in for felony with impunity. Give him a dash of brandy. So! Now he looks a little more human. What a shrimp it is, to be sure!'

For a moment he had staggered and nearly fallen, but the brandy brought a tinge of colour into his cheeks, and he sat staring with frightened eyes at his accuser.

'I have almost every link in my hands, and all the proofs which I could possibly need, so there is little which you need tell me. Still, that little may as well be cleared up to make the case complete. You had heard, Ryder, of this blue stone of the Countess of Morcar's?'

'It was Catherine Cusack who told me of it,' said he in a crackling voice.

'I see – her ladyship's waiting-maid. Well, the temptation of sudden wealth so easily acquired was too much for you, as it has been for better men before you; but you were not very scrupulous in the means you used. It seems to me, Ryder, that there is the making of a very pretty villain in you. You knew that this man Horner, the plumber, had been concerned in some such matter before, and that suspicion would rest the more readily upon him. What did you do, then? You made some small job in my lady's room – you and your confederate Cusack – and you managed that he should be the man sent for. Then, when he had left, you rifled the jewel-case, raised the alarm, and had this unfortunate man arrested. You then – '

Ryder threw himself down suddenly upon the rug and clutched at my companion's knees. 'For God's sake, have mercy!' he shrieked. 'Think of my father! Of my mother! It would break their hearts. I never went wrong before! I never will again. I swear it. I'll swear it on a Bible. Oh, don't bring it into court! For Christ's sake, don't!'

'Get back into your chair!' said Holmes sternly. 'It is very well to cringe and crawl now, but you thought little enough of this poor Horner in the dock for a crime of which he knew nothing.'

'I will fly, Mr Holmes. I will leave the country, sir. Then

the charge against him will break down.'

'Hum! We will talk about that. And now let us hear a true account of the next act. How came the stone into the goose, and how came the goose into the open market? Tell us the truth, for there lies your only hope of safety.'

Ryder passed his tongue over his parched lips. 'I will tell you it just as it happened, sir,' said he. 'When Horner had been arrested, it seemed to me that it would be best for me to get away with the stone at once, for I did not know at what moment the police might not take it into their heads to search me and my room. There was no place about the hotel where it would be safe. I went out, as if on some commission, and I made for my sister's house. She had married a man named Oakshott, and lived in Brixton Road, where she fattened fowls for the market. All the way there every man I met seemed to me to be a policeman or a detective; and, for all that it was a cold night, the sweat was pouring down my face before I came to the Brixton Road. My sister asked me what was the matter, and why I was so pale; but I told her that I had been upset by the jewel robbery at the hotel. Then I went into the back yard and smoked a pipe and wondered what it would be best to do.

'I had a friend once called Maudsley, who went to the bad, and has just been serving his time in Pentonville. One day he had met me, and fell into talk about the ways of thieves, and how they could get rid of what they stole. I knew that he would be true to me, for I knew one or two things about him; so I made up my mind to go right on to Kilburn, where he lived, and take him into my confidence. He would show me how to turn the stone into money. But how to get to him in safety? I thought of the agonies I had gone through in coming from the hotel. I might at any moment be seized and searched, and there would be the stone in my waistcoat pocket. I was leaning against the wall at the time and looking at the geese which were waddling about round my feet, and suddenly an idea came into my head which showed me how I could beat the best detective that ever lived.

'My sister had told me some weeks before that I might have the pick of her geese for a Christmas present, and I knew that she was always as good as her word. I would take my goose now, and in it I would carry my stone to Kilburn. There was a little shed in the yard, and behind this I drove one of the birds – a fine big one, white, with a barred tail. I caught it, and prying its bill open, I thrust the stone down its throat as far as my finger could reach. The bird gave a gulp, and I felt the stone pass along its gullet and down into its crop. But the creature flapped and struggled, and out came my sister to know what was the matter. As I turned to speak to her the brute broke loose and fluttered off among the others.

'"Whatever were you doing with that bird, Jem?" says she.

'"Well," said I, "you said you'd give me one for Christmas, and I was feeling which was the fattest."

'"Oh," says she, "we've set yours aside for you – Jem's bird, we call it. It's the big white one over yonder. There's twenty-six of them, which makes one for you, and one for us, and two dozen for the market."

'"Thank you, Maggie," says I; "but if it is all the same to you, I'd rather have that one I was handling just now."

'"The other is a good three pound heavier," said she, "and we fattened it expressly for you."

'"Never mind. I'll have the other, and I'll take it now," said I.

'"Oh, just as you like," said she, a little huffed. "Which is it you want, then?"

'"That white one with the barred tail, right in the middle of the flock."

'"Oh, very well. Kill it and take it with you."

'Well, I did what she said, Mr Holmes, and I carried the bird all the way to Kilburn. I told my pal what I had done, for he was a man that it was easy to tell a thing like that to. He laughed until he choked, and we got a knife and opened the goose. My heart turned to water, for there was no sign of the stone, and I knew that some terrible mistake had occurred. I left the bird, rushed back to my sister's, and hurried into the back yard. There was not a bird to be seen there.

'"Where are they all, Maggie?" I cried.

'"Gone to the dealer's, Jem."

'"Which dealer's?"

'"Breckinridge, of Covent Garden."

'"But was there another with a barred tail?" I asked, "the same as the one I chose?"

'"Yes, Jem; there were two barred-tailed ones, and I could never tell them apart."

'Well, then, of course I saw it all, and I ran off as hard as my feet would carry me to this man Breckinridge; but he had sold the lot at once, and not one word would he tell me as to where they had gone. You heard him yourselves to-night. Well, he has always answered me like that. My sister thinks that I am going mad. Sometimes I think that I am myself. And now – and now I am myself a branded thief, without ever having touched the wealth for which I sold my character. God help me! God help me!' He burst into convulsive sobbing, with his face buried in his hands.

There was a long silence, broken only by his heavy breathing and by the measured tapping of Sherlock Holmes' finger-tips upon the edge of the table. Then my friend rose and threw open the door.

'Get out!' said he.

'What, sir! Oh, Heaven bless you!'

'No more words. Get out!'

And no more words were needed. There was a rush, a clatter upon the stairs, the bang of a door, and the crisp rattle of running footfalls from the street.

'After all, Watson,' said Holmes, reaching up his hand for his clay pipe, 'I am not retained by the police to supply their deficiencies. If Horner were in danger it would be another thing; but this fellow will not appear against him, and the case must collapse. I suppose that I am commuting a felony, but it is just possible that I am saving a soul. This fellow will not go wrong again; he is too terribly frightened. Send him to gaol now, and you make him a gaol-bird for life. Besides, it is the season of forgiveness. Chance has put in our way a most singular and whimsical problem, and its solution is its own reward. If you will have the goodness to touch the bell, Doctor, we will begin another investigation, in which, also a bird will be the chief feature.'

The Invisible Man

G. K. Chesterton

In the cool blue twilight of two steep streets in Camden Town, the shop at the corner, a confectioner's, glowed like the butt of a cigar. One should rather say, perhaps, like the butt of a firework, for the light was of many colours and some complexity, broken up by many mirrors and dancing on many gilt and gaily-coloured cakes and sweetmeats. Against this one fiery glass were glued the noses of many gutter-snipes, for the chocolates were all wrapped in those red and gold and green metallic colours which are almost better than chocolate itself; and the huge white wedding-cake in the window was somehow at once remote and satisfying, just as if the whole North Pole were good to eat. Such rainbow provocations could naturally collect the youth of the neighbourhood up to the ages of ten or twelve. But this corner was also attractive to youth at a later stage; and a young man, not less than twenty-four, was staring into the same shop window. To him, also, the shop was of fiery charm, but this attraction was not wholly to be explained by chocolates; which, however, he was far from despising.

He was a tall, burly, red-haired young man, with a resolute face but a listless manner. He carried under his arm a flat, grey portfolio of black-and-white sketches which he had sold with more or less success to publishers ever since his uncle (who was an admiral) had disinherited him for Socialism, because of a lecture which he had delivered against that economic theory. His name was John Turnbull Angus.

Entering at last, he walked through the confectioner's shop into the back room, which was a sort of pastry-cook restaurant, merely raising his hat to the young lady who was serving there. She was a dark, elegant, alert girl in black, with a high colour and very quick, dark eyes; and after the ordinary interval she followed him into the inner room to take his order.

His order was evidently a usual one. 'I want, please,' he said with precision, 'one halfpenny bun and a small cup of black coffee.' An instant before the girl could turn away he added, 'Also, I want you to marry me.'

The young lady of the shop stiffened suddenly, and said: 'Those are jokes I don't allow.'

The red-haired young man lifted grey eyes of an unexpected gravity.

'Really and truly,' he said, 'it's as serious – as serious as the halfpenny bun. It is expensive, like the bun; one pays for it. It is indigestible, like the bun. It hurts.'

The dark young lady had never taken her dark eyes off him, but seemed to be studying him with almost tragic exactitude. At the end of her scrutiny she had something like the shadow of a smile, and she sat down in a chair.

'Don't you think,' observed Angus, absently, 'that it's rather cruel to eat these halfpenny buns? They might grow up into penny buns. I shall give up these brutal sports when we are married.'

The dark young lady rose from her chair and walked to the window, evidently in a state of strong but not unsympathetic cogitation. When at last she swung round again with an air of resolution, she was bewildered to observe that the young man was carefully laying out on the table various objects from the shop-window. They included a pyramid of highly coloured sweets, several plates of sandwiches, and the two decanters containing that mysterious port and sherry which are peculiar to pastry-cooks. In the middle of this neat arrangement he had carefully let down the enormous load of white sugared cake which had been the huge ornament of the window.

'What on earth are you doing?' she asked.

'Duty, my dear Laura,' he began.

'Oh, for the Lord's sake, stop a minute,' she cried, 'and don't talk to me in that way. I mean what is all that?'

'A ceremonial meal, Miss Hope.'

'And what is *that*?' she asked impatiently, pointing to the mountain of sugar.

'The wedding-cake, Mrs Angus,' he said.

The girl marched to that article, removed it with some clatter, and put it back in the shop-window; she then returned, and, putting her elegant elbows on the table, regarded the young man not unfavourably, but with considerable exasperation.

'You don't give me any time to think,' she said.

'I'm not such a fool,' he answered; 'that's my Christian humility.'

She was still looking at him; but she had grown considerably graver behind the smile.

'Mr Angus,' she said steadily, 'before there is a minute more of this nonsense I must tell you something about myself as shortly as I can.'

'Delighted,' replied Angus gravely. 'You might tell me something about myself, too, while you are about it.'

'Oh, do hold your tongue and listen,' she said. 'It's nothing that I'm ashamed of, and it isn't even anything that I'm specially sorry about. But what would you say if there were something that is no business of mine and yet is my nightmare?'

'In that case,' said the man seriously, 'I should suggest that you bring back the cake.'

'Well, you must listen to the story first,' said Laura persistently. 'To begin with, I must tell you that my father owned the inn called the "Red Fish" at Ludbury, and I used to serve people in the bar.'

'I have often wondered,' he said, 'why there was a kind of a Christian air about this one confectioner's shop.'

'Ludbury is a sleepy, grassy little hole in the Eastern Counties, and the only kind of people who ever came to the "Red Fish" were occasional commercial travellers, and for the rest, the most awful people you can see, only you've never seen them. I mean little, loungy men, who had just enough to live on, and had nothing to do but lean about in bar-rooms and bet on horses, in bad clothes that were just too good for them. Even these wretched young rotters were not very common at our house; but there were two of them that were a lot too common – common in every sort of way. They both lived on money of their own, and were wearisomely idle and over-dressed. But yet I was a bit sorry for them, because I half believe they slunk into our little empty bar because each of them had a slight deformity; the sort of thing that some yokels laugh at. It wasn't exactly a deformity either; it was more an oddity. One of them was a surprisingly small man, something like a dwarf, or at least like a jockey. He was not at all jockeyish to look at, though, he had a round black head and a well-trimmed black beard, bright eyes like a bird's; he jingled money in his pockets; he jangled a great gold watch chain; and he never turned up except dressed just too much like a gentleman to be one. He was no fool, though, though a futile idler; he was curiously clever at all kinds of things that couldn't be the slightest use; a sort of impromptu conjuring; making fifteen matches set fire to each other like a regular firework; or cutting a banana or some such thing into a dancing doll. His name was Isidore Smythe; and I can see him still, with his little dark face, just coming up to the counter, making a jumping kangaroo out of five cigars.

'The other fellow was more silent and more ordinary; but somehow he alarmed me much more than poor little Smythe. He was very tall and slight, and light-haired; his nose had a high bridge, and he might almost have been handsome in a spectral sort of way; but he had one of the most appalling squints I have ever seen or heard of. When he looked straight at you, you didn't know where you were yourself, let alone what he was looking at. I fancy this sort of disfigurement embittered the poor chap a little; for while Smythe was ready to show off his monkey tricks anywhere, James Welkin (that was the squinting man's name) never did anything except soak in our bar parlour, and go for great walks by himself in the flat, grey country all round. All the same, I think Smythe, too, was a little sensitive about being so small, though he carried it off more smartly. And so it was that I was really puzzled, as well as startled, and very sorry, when they both offered to marry me in the same week.

'Well, I did what I've since thought was perhaps a silly thing. But, after all, these freaks were my friends in a way; and I had a horror of their thinking I refused them for the real reason, which was that they were so impossibly ugly. So I made up some gas of another sort, about never meaning to marry anyone who hadn't carved his way in the world. I said it was a point of principle with me not to live on money that was just inherited like theirs. Two days after I had talked in this well-meaning sort of way, the whole trouble began. The first thing I heard was that both of them had gone off to seek their fortunes, as if they were in some silly fairy tale.

'Well, I've never seen either of them from that day to this. But I've had two letters from the little man called Smythe, and really they were rather exciting.'

'Ever heard of the other man?' asked Angus.

'No, he never wrote,' said the girl, after an instant's hesitation. 'Smythe's first letter was simply to say that he had started out walking with Welkin to London; but Welkin was such a good walker that the little man dropped out of it, and took a rest by the roadside. He happened to be picked up by some travelling show, and, partly because he was nearly a dwarf, and partly because he was really a clever little wretch, he got on quite well in the show business, and was soon sent up to the Aquarium, to do some tricks that I forgot. That was his first letter. His second was much more of a startler, and I only got it last week.'

The man called Angus emptied his coffee-cup and regarded her with mild and patient eyes. Her own mouth took a slight twist of laughter as she resumed: 'I suppose you've seen on the hoardings all about this "Smythe's Silent Service"? Or you must be the only person that hasn't. Oh, I don't know much about it, it's some clock-work invention for doing all the housework by machinery. You know the sort of thing: "Press a button – A Butler who Never Drinks". "Turn a handle – Ten Housemaids who Never Flirt". You must have seen the advertisements. Well, whatever these machines are, they are making pots of money; and they are making it all for that little imp whom I knew down in Ludbury. I can't help feeling pleased the poor little chap has fallen on his feet; but the plain fact is, I'm in terror of his turning up any minute and telling me he's carved his way in the world – as he certainly has.'

'And the other man?' repeated Angus with a sort of obstinate quietude.

Laura Hope got to her feet suddenly. 'My friend,' she said: 'I think you are a witch. Yes, you are quite right. I have not seen a line of the other man's writing; and I have no more notion than the dead of what or where he is. But it is of him that I am frightened. It is he who is all about my path. It is he who has half driven me mad. Indeed, I think he has driven me mad; for I have felt him where he could not have been, and I have heard his voice when he could not have spoken.'

'Well, my dear,' said the young man, cheerfully, 'if he were Satan himself, he is done for now you have told somebody. One goes mad all alone, old girl. But when was it you fancied you felt and heard our squinting friend?'

'I heard James Welkin laugh as plainly as I hear you speak,' said the girl, steadily. 'There was nobody there, for I stood just outside the shop at the corner, and could see down both streets at once. I had forgotten how he laughed, though his laugh was as odd as his squint. I had not thought of him for nearly a year. But it's a solemn truth that a few seconds later the first letter came from his rival.'

'Did you ever make the spectre speak or squeak, or anything?' asked Angus, with some interest.

Laura suddenly shuddered, and then said with an unshaken voice: 'Yes. Just when I had finished reading the second letter from Isidore Smythe announcing his success, just then, I heard Welkin say: "He shan't have you, though." It was quite plain, as if he were in the room. It is awful; I think I must be mad.'

'If you really were mad,' said the young man, 'you would think you must be sane. But certainly there seems to me to be something a little rum about this unseen gentleman. Two heads are better than one – I spare you allusions to any other organs – and really, if you would allow me, as a sturdy, practical man, to bring back the wedding-cake out of the window – '

Even as he spoke, there was a sort of steely shriek in the street outside, and a small motor, driven at devilish speed, shot up to the door of the shop and stuck there. In the same flash of time a small man in a shiny top hat stood stamping in the outer room.

Angus, who had hitherto maintained hilarious ease from motives of mental hygiene, revealed the strain of his soul by striding abruptly out of the inner room and confronting the newcomer. A glance at him was quite sufficient to confirm the savage guesswork of a man in love. This very dapper but dwarfish figure, with the spike of black beard carried insolently forward, the clever unrestful eyes, the neat but very nervous fingers, could be none other than the man just described to him: Isidore Smythe, who made dolls out of banana skins and matchboxes: Isidore Smythe, who made millions out of undrinking butlers and unflirting housemaids of metal. For a moment the two men, instinctively understanding each other's air of possession, looked at each other with that curious cold generosity which is the soul of rivalry.

Mr Smythe, however, made no allusion to the ultimate ground of their antagonism, but said simply and explosively: 'Has Miss Hope seen that thing on the window?'

'On the window?' repeated the staring Angus.

'There's no time to explain other things,' said the small millionaire shortly. 'There's some tomfoolery going on here that has to be investigated.'

He pointed his polished walking-stick at the window, recently depleted by the bridal preparations of Mr Angus; and that gentleman was astonished to see along the front of the glass a long strip of paper pasted, which had certainly not been on the window when he had looked through it some time before. Following the energetic Smythe outside into the street, he found that some yard and a half of stamp paper had been carefully gummed along the glass outside, and on this was written in straggly characters: 'If you marry Smythe, he will die.'

'Laura,' said Angus, putting his big red head into the shop, 'you're not mad.'

'It's the writing of that fellow Welkin,' said Smythe gruffly. 'I haven't seen him for years, but he's always bothering me. Five times in the last fortnight he's had threatening letters left at my flat, and I can't even find out who leaves them, let alone if it is Welkin himself. The porter of the flats swears that no suspicious characters have been seen, and here he has pasted up a sort of dado on a public shop window, while the people in the shop – '

'Quite so,' said Angus modestly, 'while the people in the shop were having tea. Well, sir, I can assure you I appreciate your common sense in dealing so directly with the matter. We can talk about other things afterwards. The fellow cannot be very far off yet, for I swear there was no paper there when I went last to the window, ten or fifteen minutes ago. On the other hand, he's too far off to be chased, as we don't even know the direction. If you'll take my advice, Mr Smythe, you'll put this at once in the hands of some energetic inquiry man, private rather than public. I know an extremely clever fellow, who has set up in business five minutes from here in your car. His name's Flambeau, and though his youth was a bit stormy, he's a strictly honest man now, and his brains are worth money. He lives in Lucknow Mansions, Hampstead.'

'That is odd,' said the little man, arching his black eyebrows. 'I live myself in Himalaya Mansions round the corner. Perhaps you might care to come with me; I can go to my rooms and sort out these queer Welkin documents, while you run round and get your friend the detective.'

'You are very good,' said Angus politely. 'Well, the sooner we act the better.'

Both men, with a queer kind of impromptu fairness, took the same sort of formal farewell of the lady, and both jumped into the brisk little car. As Smythe took the wheel and they turned the great corner of the street, Angus was amused to see a gigantesque poster of 'Smythe's Silent Service', with a picture of a huge headless iron doll, carrying a saucepan with the legend, 'A Cook Who is Never Cross'.

'I use them in my own flat,' said the little black-bearded man, laughing, 'partly for advertisement, and partly for real convenience. Honestly, and all above board, those big clockwork dolls of mine do bring you coals or claret or a time-table quicker than any live servants I've ever known, if you know which knob to press. But I'll never deny, between ourselves, that such servants have their disadvantages, too.'

'Indeed,' said Angus; 'is there something they can't do?'

'Yes,' replied Smythe coolly; 'they can't tell me who left those threatening letters at my flat.'

The man's motor was small and swift like himself; in fact, like his domestic service, it was of his own invention. If he was an advertising quack, he was one who believed in his own wares. The sense of something tiny and flying was accentuated as they swept up long white curves of road in the dead but open daylight of evening. Soon the white curves came sharper and dizzier; they were upon ascending spirals, as they say in the modern religions. For, indeed, they were cresting a corner of London which is almost as precipitous as Edinburgh, if not quite so pictur-esque. Terrace rose above terrace, and the special tower of flats they sought, rose above them all to almost Egyptian height, gilt by the level sunset. The change, as they turned the corner and entered the crescent known as Himalaya Mansions, was as abrupt as the opening of a window; for they found that pile of flats sitting above London as above a green sea of slate. Opposite to the mansions, on the other side of the gravel crescent, was a bushy enclo-sure more like a steep hedge or dyke than a garden, and some way below that ran a strip of artificial water, a sort of canal, like the moat of that embowered fortress. As the car swept round the crescent it passed, at one corner, the stray stall of a man selling chestnuts; and right away at the other end of the curve, Angus could see a dim blue police-man walking slowly. These were the only human shapes in that high suburban solitude; but he had an irrational sense that they expressed the speechless poetry of London. He felt as if they were figures in a story.

The little car shot up to the right house like a bullet, and shot out its owner like a bomb shell. He was immediately inquiring of a tall commissionaire in shining braid, and a short porter in shirt sleeves, whether anybody or anything had been seeking his apartments. He was assured that nobody and nothing had passed these officials since his last inquiries; whereupon he and the slightly bewildered Angus were shot up in the lift like a rocket, till they reached the top floor.

'Just come in for a minute,' said the breathless Smythe. 'I want to show you those Welkin letters. Then you might run round the corner and fetch your friend.' He pressed a button concealed in the wall, and the door opened of itself.

It opened on a long, commodious ante-room, of which the only arresting features, ordinarily speaking, were the rows of tall half-human mechanical figures that stood up on both sides like tailors' dummies. Like tailors' dummies they were headless; and like tailors' dummies they had a handsome unnecessary humpiness in the shoulders, and a pigeon-breasted protuberance of chest; but barring this, they were not much more like a human figure than any automatic machine at a station that is about the human height. They had two great hooks like arms, for carrying trays; and they were painted pea-green, or vermilion, or black for convenience of distinction; in every other way they were only automatic machines and nobody would have looked twice at them. On this occasion, at least, nobody did. For between the two rows of these domestic dummies lay something more interesting than most of the mechanics of the world. It was a white, tattered scrap of paper scrawled with red ink; and the agile inventor had snatched it up almost as soon as the door flew open. He handed it to Angus without a word. The red ink on it actually was not dry, and the message ran: 'If you have been to see her today, I shall kill you.'

There was a short silence, and then Isidore Smythe said quietly: 'Would you like a little whisky? I rather feel as if I should.'

'Thank you; I should like a little Flambeau,' said Angus, gloomily. 'This business seems to me to be getting rather grave. I'm going round at once to fetch him.'

'Right you are,' said the other, with admirable cheerfulness. 'Bring him round here as quick as you can.'

But as Angus closed the front door behind him he saw Smythe push back a button, and one of the clockwork images glided from its place and slid along a groove in the floor carrying a tray with syphon and decanter. There did seem something a trifle weird about leaving the little man alone among those dead servants, who were coming to life as the door closed.

Six steps down from Smythe's landing the man in shirt sleeves was doing something with a pail. Angus stopped to extract a promise, fortified with a prospective bribe, that he would remain in that place until the return with the detective, and would keep count of any kind of stranger coming up those stairs. Dashing down to the front hall he then laid similar charges of vigilance on the commissionaire at the front door, from whom he learned the simplifying circumstance that there was no back door. Not content with this, he captured the floating policeman and induced him to stand opposite the entrance and watch it; and finally paused an instant for a pennyworth of chestnuts, and an inquiry as to the probable length of the merchant's stay in the neighbourhood.

The chestnut seller, turning up the collar of his coat, told him he should probably be moving shortly, as he thought it was going to snow. Indeed, the evening was growing grey and bitter, but Angus, with all his eloquence, proceeded to nail the chestnut man to his post.

'Keep yourself warm on your own chestnuts,' he said earnestly. 'Eat up your whole stock; I'll make it worth your while. I'll give you a sovereign if you'll wait here till I come back, and then tell me whether any man, woman, or child has gone into that house where the commissionaire is standing.'

He then walked away smartly, with a last look at the besieged tower.

'I've made a ring round that room, anyhow,' he said. They can't all four of them be Mr Welkin's accomplices.'

Lucknow Mansions were, so to speak, on a lower platform of that hill of houses, of which Himalaya Mansions might be called the peak. Mr Flambeau's semi-official flat was on the ground floor, and presented in every way a marked contrast to the American machinery and cold hotel-like luxury of the flat of the Silent Service. Flambeau, who was a friend of Angus, received him in a rococo artistic den behind his office, of which the ornaments were sabres, harque-buses, Eastern curiosities, flasks of Italian wine, savage cooking-pots, a plumy Persian cat, and a small dusty-looking Roman Catholic priest, who looked particularly out of place.

'This is my friend, Father Brown,' said Flambeau. 'I've often wanted you to meet him. Splendid weather, this; a little cold for Southerners like me.'

'Yes, I think it will keep clear,' said Angus, sitting down on a violet-striped Eastern ottoman.

'No,' said the priest quietly; 'it has begun to snow.'

And indeed, as he spoke, the first few flakes, foreseen by the man of chestnuts, began to drift across the darkening window-pane.

'Well,' said Angus heavily. 'I'm afraid I've come on business, and rather jumpy business at that. The fact is, Flambeau, within a stone's throw of your house is a fellow who badly wants your help; he's perpetually being haunted and threatened by an invisible enemy – a scoundrel whom nobody has even seen.' As Angus proceeded to tell the whole tale of Smythe and Welkin beginning with Laura's story, and going on with his own, the supernatural laugh at the corner of two empty streets, the strange distinct words spoken in an empty room, Flambeau grew more and more vividly concerned, and the little priest seemed to be left out of it, like a piece of furniture. When it came to the scribbled stamp paper pasted on the window, Flambeau rose, seeming to fill the room with his huge shoulders.

'If you don't mind,' he said, 'I think you had better tell me the rest on the nearest road to this man's house. It strikes me, somehow, that there is no time to be lost.'

'Delighted,' said Angus, rising also, 'though he's safe enough for the present, for I've set four men to watch the only hole to his burrow.'

They turned out into the street, the small priest trundling after them with the docility of a small dog. He merely said, in a cheerful way, like one making conversation: 'How quick the snow gets thick on the ground.'

As they threaded the steep side streets already powdered with silver, Angus finished his story; and by the time they reached the crescent with the towering flats, he had leisure to turn his attention to the four sentinels. The chestnut seller, both before and after receiving a sovereign, swore stubbornly that he had watched the door and seen no visitor enter. The policeman was even more emphatic. He said he had had experience of crooks of all kinds, in top hats and in rags; he wasn't so green as to expect suspicious characters to look suspicious; he looked out for anybody, and, so help him, there had been nobody. And when all three men gathered round the gilded commissionaire, who still stood smiling astride of the porch, the verdict was more final still.

'I've got a right to ask any man, duke or dustman, what he wants in these flats,' said the genial and gold-laced giant, 'and I'll swear there's been nobody to ask since this gentleman went away.'

The unimportant Father Brown, who stood back, looking modestly at the pavement, here ventured to say meekly: 'Has nobody been up and down stairs, then, since the snow began to fall? It began while we were all round at Flambeau's.'

'Nobody's been in here, sir, you can take it from me,' said the official, with beaming authority.

'Then I wonder what that is?' said the priest, and stared at the ground blankly like a fish.

The others all looked down also; and Flambeau used a fierce exclamation and a French gesture. For it was unquestionably true that down the middle of the entrance guarded by the man in gold lace, actually between the arrogant, stretched legs of that colossus, ran a stringy pattern of grey footprints stamped upon the white snow.

'God!' cried Angus involuntarily; 'the Invisible Man!'

Without another word he turned and dashed up the stairs, with Flambeau following; but Father Brown still stood looking about him in the snow-clad street as if he had lost interest in his query.

Flambeau was plainly in a mood to break down the door with his big shoulder; but the Scotsman, with more reason, if less intuition, fumbled about on the frame of the door till he found the invisible button; and the door swung slowly open.

It showed substantially the same serried interior; the hall had grown darker, though it was still struck here and there with the last crimson shafts of sunset, and one or two of the headless machines had been moved from their places for this or that purpose, and stood here and there about the twilit place. The green and red of their coats were all darkened in the dusk, and their likeness to human shapes slightly increased by their very shapelessness. But in the middle of them all, exactly where the paper with the red ink had lain, there lay something that looked very like red ink spilled out of its bottle. But it was not red ink.

With a French combination of reason and violence Flambeau simply said 'Murder!' and, plunging into the flat, had explored every corner and cupboard of it in five minutes. But if he expected to find a corpse he found none.

Isidore Smythe simply was not in the place, either dead or alive. After the most tearing search the two men met each other in the outer hall with streaming faces and staring eyes. 'My friend,' said Flambeau, talking French in his excitement, 'not only is your murderer invisible, but he makes invisible also the murdered man.'

Angus looked round at the dim room full of dummies, and in some Celtic corner of his Scotch soul a shudder started. One of the life-size dolls stood immediately over-shadowing the blood stain, summoned, perhaps, by the slain man an instant before he fell. One of the high-shoul-dered hooks that served the thing for arms, was a little lifted and Angus had suddenly the horrid fancy that poor Smythe's own iron child had struck him down. Matter had rebelled, and these machines had killed their master. But even so, what had they done with him?

'Eaten him?' said the nightmare at his ear; and he sick-ened for an instant at the idea of rent, human remains absorbed and crushed into all the acephalous clockwork.

He recovered his mental health by an emphatic effort, and said to Flambeau: 'Well, there it is. The poor fellow has evaporated like a cloud and left a red streak on the floor. The tale does not belong to this world.'

'There is only one thing to be done,' said Flambeau, 'whether it belongs to this world or the other, I must go down and talk to my friend.'

They descended, passing the man with the pail, who again asseverated that he had let no intruder pass, down to the commissionaire and the hovering chestnut man, who rightly reasserted their own watchfulness. But when Angus looked round for his fourth confirmation he could not see it, and called out with some nervousness: 'Where is the policeman?'

'I beg your pardon,' said Father Brown; 'that is my fault. I just sent him down the road to investigate something – that I just thought worth investigating.'

'Well, we want him back pretty soon,' said Angus abruptly, 'for the wretched man upstairs has not only been murdered, but wiped out.'

'How?' asked the priest.

'Father,' said Flambeau, after a pause, 'upon my soul I believe it is more in your department than mine. No friend or foe has entered the house, but Smythe is gone, as if stolen by the fairies. If that is not supernatural, I – '

As he spoke they were all checked by an unusual sight; the big blue policeman came round the corner of the crescent running. He came straight up to Brown.

'You're right, sir,' he panted, 'they've just found poor Mr Smythe's body in the canal down below.'

Angus put his hand wildly to his head. 'Did he run down and drown himself?' he asked.

'He never came down, I'll swear,' said the constable,

'and he wasn't drowned either, for he died of a great stab over the heart.'

'And yet you saw no one enter?' said Flambeau in a grave voice.

'Let us walk down the road a little,' said the priest.

As they reached the other end of the crescent he observed abruptly: 'Stupid of me! I forgot to ask the policeman something. I wonder if they found a light brown sack.'

'Why a light brown sack?' asked Angus, astonished.

'Because if it was any other coloured sack, the case must begin over again,' said Father Brown; 'but if it was a light brown sack, why, the case is finished.'

'I am pleased to hear it,' said Angus with hearty irony. 'It hasn't begun, so far as I am concerned.'

'You must tell us all about it,' said Flambeau, with a strange heavy simplicity, like a child.

Unconsciously they were walking with quickening steps down the long sweep of road on the other side of the high crescent, Father Brown leading briskly, though in silence. At last he said with an almost touching vagueness: 'Well, I'm afraid you'll think it so prosy. We always begin at the abstract end of things, and you can't begin this story anywhere else.

'Have you ever noticed this – that people never answer what you say? They answer what you mean – or what they think you mean. Suppose one lady says to another in a country house, "Is anybody staying with you?" the lady doesn't answer "Yes; the butler, the three footmen, the parlour-maid, and so on," though the parlour-maid may be in the room, or the butler behind her chair. She says: "There is *nobody* staying with us," meaning nobody of the sort you mean. But suppose a doctor inquiring into an epidemic asks, "Who is staying in the house?" then the lady will remember the butler, the parlour-maid, and the rest. All language is used like that; you never get a question answered literally, even when you get it answered truly. When those four quite honest men said that no man had gone into the Mansions, they did not really mean that *no man* had gone into them. They meant no man whom they could suspect of being your man. A man did go into the house, and did come out of it, but they never noticed him.'

'An invisible man?' inquired Angus, raising his red eyebrows.

'A mentally invisible man,' said Father Brown.

A minute or two after he resumed in the same un-assuming voice, like a man thinking his way. 'Of course, you can't think of such a man, until you do think of him. That's where his cleverness comes in. But I came to think of him through two or three little things in the tale Mr Angus told us. First, there was the fact that this Welkin went for long walks. And then there was the vast lot of stamp paper on the window. And then, most of all, there were the two things the young lady said – things that couldn't be true. Don't get annoyed,' he added hastily, noting a sudden movement of the Scotsman's head; 'she thought they were true all right, but they couldn't be true. A person *can't* be quite alone in a street a second before she receives a letter. She can't be quite alone in a street when she starts reading a letter just received. There must be somebody pretty near her; he must be mentally invisible.'

'Why must there be somebody near her?' asked Angus.

'Because,' said Father Brown: 'barring carrier-pigeons, somebody must have brought her the letter.'

'Do you really mean to say,' asked Flambeau, with energy, 'that Welkin carried his rival's letters to his lady?'

'Yes,' said the priest. 'Welkin carried his rival's letters to his lady. You see, he had to.'

'Oh, I can't stand much more of this,' exploded Flambeau. 'Who is this fellow? What does he look like? What is the usual get-up of a mentally invisible man?'

'He is dressed rather handsomely in red, blue and gold,' replied the priest promptly with decision, 'and in this striking, and even showy costume he entered Himalaya Mansions under eight human eyes; he killed Smythe in cold blood, and came down into the street again carrying the dead body in his arms – '

'Reverend sir,' cried Angus, standing still, 'are you raving mad, or am I?'

'You are not mad,' said Brown, 'only a little unobservant. You have not noticed such a man as this, for example.'

He took three quick strides forward, and put his hand on the shoulder of an ordinary passing postman who had bustled by them unnoticed under the shade of the trees.

'Nobody ever notices postmen, somehow,' he said thoughtfully; 'yet they have passions like other men, and even carry large bags where a small corpse can be stowed quite easily.'

The postman, instead of turning naturally, had ducked and tumbled against the garden fence. He was a lean fair-bearded man of very ordinary appearance, but as he turned an alarmed face over his shoulder, all three men were fixed with an almost fiendish squint.

Flambeau went back to his sabres, purple rugs and Persian cat, having many things to attend to. John Turnbull Angus went back to the lady at the shop, with whom that imprudent young man contrives to be extremely comfortable. But Father Brown walked those snow-covered hills under the stars for many hours with a murderer, and what they said to each other will never be known.

Cinders

A Rebus Story for Christmas

Ian Rankin

The Fairy Godmother was dead.

Rebus had had to fight his way through the throng of rubber-neckers outside the Theatre Royal. It was early evening, dark and drizzling, but they didn't seem to mind. He showed his warrant card to a uniformed officer at the cordon, and then again as he entered the red-carpeted foyer. The doors to the auditorium were open, the remaining audience members grumbling in that Edinburgh way as they queued to give their contact details before being allowed to leave. The curtain had been raised for the show's second act, revealing the kitchen of some grand house or castle, all fake stone walls and glowing fireplace.

'Apparently,' a voice next to Rebus announced, 'there's a bit of slapstick with Buttons as he tries baking a cake.'

'Shaving-foam in the face?' Rebus guessed.

'That sort of thing.' Detective Inspector Siobhan Clarke managed a thin smile.

The youngest members of the audience were setting up cries of protest, their annual panto treat ruined. Parents looked numbed, some of the mothers dabbing away tears.

'They know?' Rebus said.

'Second half doesn't start, police arrive – I'd say they've guessed there's no happy ending.'

'So what happened?'

'Easier if I show you.' She turned back into the foyer and pushed open a door marked Private. Stairs up, a narrow corridor, then another door, more stairs, and turns to left and right.

'Should we be leaving a trail of breadcrumbs?' Rebus inquired.

'Wrong story,' Clarke answered.

She had to knock at a final door. It was opened by a uniformed officer. They were in another corridor with doors off.

'Make-up, wardrobe, dressing rooms,' Clarke intoned.

'The business of show.' Rebus peered into some of the rooms as they passed them. Rails festooned with gaudy clothing, strip-lit mirrors, props and wigs. There were loud-speakers set into the walls, broadcasting the sounds from the auditorium. The Scene of Crime crew were bagging and tagging.

'We're not worried about contamination?' Rebus checked.

'Twenty or thirty people pass this way a dozen or more times per show. Maxtone doesn't think we'd be adding much to the mix.'

'Doug Maxtone is in charge?'

'How do you not know that?' Clarke stopped in her tracks.

'I was just passing, Siobhan.'

'Just passing?'

'Well, maybe I heard something at the station …'

'But you're not on the team?' She rolled her eyes at the stupidity of her own question. 'Of course not – Doug Maxtone's hardly in your fan club.'

'I can't understand it – we've got badges and everything.'

'This is a murder inquiry, John. You don't just walk in.'

'Yet here I am.' Rebus gave a shrug. 'So why not show me where it happened?'

She sighed as she made up her mind, then led the way. 'We can't go in, not without being suited up.'

'Understood.'

So they stood at the threshold instead. The interior seemed frozen in the moment. Vases of flowers and good luck cards. Bottles of water and blackcurrant cordial. A bowl of fruit. A small suitcase, lying open. A chair tipped over. A dark stain on the pale blue carpet.

'I smell smoke.'

'Not quite enough to set off the alarm,' Clarke said. 'A metal waste-bin.' She nodded to where it had once sat. 'Off to the lab.'

'Was she a smoker?'

'It was paper of some kind – plus sandwich wrappers and who knows what else.'

'A blow to the head, I heard.'

'Probably when she was seated, facing the mirror. She didn't have the biggest of roles – pops up with the gown and glass slippers, then the coach. Comes on again near the end – or would have.'

'So it's the interval and she's changed out of her sparkly gown and wings?' Rebus mused. 'Meaning the costume department would have been lurking.'

'We're interviewing them.'

'How long is the interval?'

'Twenty minutes.'

'Lots of people backstage?'

'Lots.'

'She would have seen them.' He nodded towards the

mirror. 'She'd have seen whoever walked in.'

'Baron Hardup has the next dressing room along. Didn't hear any screams. Then again, he had the radio on, listening to some horse race.'

'And through the other wall?'

'Stairwell.'

'No security cameras?'

'Not here, no.' Clarke paused. 'Did you know her?'

'How do you mean?'

'She was on TV in the 70s and 80s. A couple of sitcoms, even a few films.'

'I saw her face on the poster outside. Didn't ring any bells.'

'And the name? Celia Jagger?' She watched Rebus shrug. 'You've not asked about the weapon.'

Rebus scanned the dressing room but came up empty. 'Enlighten me,' he said.

'The glass slipper,' Clarke said. 'The one left behind at the Ball …'

Not that it was a real glass slipper. It was Perspex or something similar. And it wasn't the one from the performance. The production kept two spares. One of these had been removed from the props department and used in the attack, its stiletto heel piercing Jagger's skull and killing her instantly.

The props department was basically a large walk-in cupboard with shelves. The door had a lock, but was always open during performances. There were storage boxes bearing the name of each character along with a list of contents. Rebus held one of the remaining slippers in his hand. It was heavier than he had anticipated. Nicely made, but scuffed from use. Not that an audience would notice, not with a spotlight making it shine.

Clarke had gone off somewhere, with a warning that he should 'keep his head down'. Some of the chaos had subsided. Fewer headless chickens as the inquiry found its rhythm. Twelve dressing rooms, three of them to accommodate the chorus (who doubled as dancers). The theatre had no orchestra pit – the music was pre-recorded. Two technicians ran everything from a couple of laptops. Everyone would be asked about their movements during the interval. Statements would have to be verified. As yet, no one seemed to be asking the most basic question of all: who would want Celia Jagger dead? Her killing was the end of a story, and for stories you went to people. Which was why Rebus placed the shoe back in the box marked Cinders, and walked towards the exit.

The sign said Stage Door, and that was where he eventually found himself. There was an antechamber of sorts, with a list of actors and crew fixed to its wall. Like clocking in to some old-fashioned factory job, when you arrived you slid a wooden slat along to show you were IN. From behind a glass partition, the man in the security booth watched Rebus.

'I like this,' Rebus said, pointing to the wall.

'It's been here almost as long as the building.'

'And what about you?'

'I used to build the sets. Everything was custom-made in those days.'

'And now?'

'Mostly from stock. Newcastle or somewhere does *Cinderella* one year, we'll take what we need from them the next, while our *Aladdin* might head to Aberdeen. We built the tram from scratch, mind.'

'The tram?'

'Director's idea – instead of a carriage. Big puff of smoke and there's an Edinburgh tram. Pretty clever really – means we don't need any horses. Couple of the stage hands use a pulley and Cinders is off to the ball.' The man's smile faded. 'How long will we be closed?'

'Hard to say.'

'Theatre can't go on without it. Same for a lot of these old places – a full house for a few months means you can afford to run the rest of the year.'

'Is that what happens?'

The guard nodded. He was in shirt-sleeves, a mug of tea on the desk next to him. CCTV screens showed the alleyway outside, empty auditorium, and front of house.

'I'm Detective Sergeant Rebus, by the way,' Rebus said.

'Willie Mearns.'

'How long have you been doing this job, Mr Mearns?'

'Fifteen years.'

'Ever since you retired from the workshop?' Making Mearns seventy-five, maybe even eighty. He looked sprightly though. Rebus reckoned the man's memory would be sharp. 'Have you been questioned yet?'

'Not formally – just asked if I'd seen anyone suspicious.'

'I'm guessing you said no.'

'Quite right.'

'And Celia Jagger – did you know her to talk to?'

'Oh aye. I had to remind her that I built the set when she appeared in a play here back in her heyday.'

'Did you use the word "heyday"?'

'I'm not that daft.'

'She had a bit of an ego then?'

'Most of them do. Don't get me wrong – they're lovely with it. But Celia was miffed she didn't get one of the big dressing rooms.'

'They all looked much the same to me.'

'A few inches can make all the difference.'

'You say she was "miffed" – is that as far as it went?'

'More or less.'

Rebus studied the man for a few seconds. 'There's a pub across the street. Do you know it?'

'I might have passed through its door on occasion.'

Rebus smiled. 'Well, tonight we've got half a dozen of Police Scotland's finest keeping watch on the Theatre Royal. I think you can maybe call it a day, Mr Mearns.'

The man made show of considering his options, then started rising to his feet. 'I'll drink to that,' he said.

The interviews were taking place at St Leonard's police station. Rebus found Clarke pacing a corridor, scanning transcripts.

'Who have we got?' he asked her.

She nodded in turn towards four doors. 'Tracy Sidwell, John Carrier, Robert Tennant, Jamie Salter.'

'So that's Cinderella, Baron Hardup, Prince Charming and Buttons.'

'You're well informed.'

'I just spent an hour in a pub with a man who likes to talk. Hardup's a bit too fond of the horses apparently. Always needing to borrow a few quid to tide him over.

'Meantime, Prince Charming left his wife and two kids for Cinderella – not quite a fairy tale.'

Clarke stared at him. 'Anything else?'

Rebus shrugged. 'There are whispers about Buttons

and the Wicked Stepmother. Giggles and whispers behind closed dressing-room doors. Who else have we got?'

'They're waiting in the office until we're ready for them.' They walked together to the MIT suite. The Ugly Sisters – panto stalwarts Davie Clegg and Russell Gloag – had changed out of their costumes but still bore traces of make-up. They were seated alongside the show's writer/director Maurice Welsh, who was visibly trembling as he spoke with another man. Rebus guessed this would be Alan Yates, producer and owner of the Theatre Royal. Seeing the two detectives, Yates leapt to his feet. He was in his sixties and looked to have dined out for most of them.

'Any news?' he asked.

'Not yet, sir,' Clarke assured him.

'We need to offer refunds … prep an understudy. The show must – '

'Sorry to disillusion you, sir,' Rebus butted in. 'But the theatre remains a crime scene. It doesn't open again until we say so.'

'And even then, Alan,' Welsh added tiredly, 'who's going to be in the mood? I mean the audience rather than the cast. We'll have nothing but ghouls …'

'Run's finished,' Davie Clegg agreed. 'Can't sit in that dressing-room and not think of Celia.'

Yates ran a hand through what hair he had left. 'But without the panto there *is* no Theatre Royal! It's our banker!'

'Sorry, Alan.' Clegg offered a shrug of sympathy.

'Ruined,' Yates muttered, falling back on to his seat. Maurice Welsh patted his arm.

'That's all very well,' Russell Gloag piped up, 'but it doesn't tell us who killed poor Celia. And if I find out it was any one of you.'

'Actually that's our job,' Clarke informed him. She broke off as an exhausted-looking detective filled the doorway. He checked his notepad.

'Maurice Welsh?' The director stood up, looking as if a gust might topple him. 'If you'll follow me, sir.' The detective locked eyes with Clarke and shook his head: nothing to report.

Rebus gestured for Clarke to follow him into the corridor. He checked they were out of earshot. 'Where's everyone else? The crew and chorus, plus Dandini and the Stepmother?'

'One of the other offices. Otherwise they'd have been like sardines.' She studied him. 'What else did your friend in the pub tell you?'

'Bits and pieces. I'm not sure yet what they – '

'What in God's name is *he* doing here?'

They both turned in the direction of the approaching voice. DCI Doug Maxtone seemed to fill the corridor as he strode towards them.

'I was just passing,' Rebus explained slowly. 'Happened

to bump into DI Clarke and she was just singing your praises.'

Maxtone ignored Rebus, his attention fixed on Clarke. He brandished a sheet of paper ripped from a pad. 'Forensics played a blinder,' he told her.

'The waste-bin?'

'Salient contents: one promotional photograph of Celia Jagger. Not quite done to a cinder ...'

'And?'

'It was signed.' Maxtone checked his note. "To my darling Ed with all my love".'

'Ed?' Clarke narrowed her eyes. 'Edwin Oakes?'

'AKA Dandini. Is he inside?' Maxtone was gesturing towards the MIT room.

'He's with the chorus and crew.'

Maxtone's face hardened. 'I've just come from there.'

Clarke's lips formed an O. 'No Dandini?' she surmised.

'They thought he must be here.'

Rebus made show of clearing his throat. 'Maybe he found the trap-door.'

'You're as useful as last year's turkey,' Maxtone snarled, before barrelling his way back along the corridor, Clarke at his heels.

Rebus stayed where he was. Then he took out his phone and a scrap of paper, reading Willie Mearns' number from it as he got busy on the keypad.

'I need everything there is to know about Edwin Oakes,' he said. As he listened, his eyes began to narrow and his brow furrow. *Curiouser and curiouser...*

* * *

The following morning, Rebus was at St Leonard's early. He went through the interview transcripts, gleaning bits and pieces. There was no love lost between the Ugly Sisters apparently – they worked together for the sake of the pay cheque, each privately confiding his loathing of the other to various stagehands. Wardrobe department, make-up, deputy stage manager ... all had sung for the detectives. The show's director had a history of substance abuse, as did Prince Charming. Buttons was notoriously lazy, and had almost come to blows with both director and producer while attempting to cut back on his lines so he wouldn't have to remember them. He would also ad lib weak jokes, meaning more arguments after each and every performance.

But there was plenty of gossip about the crew, too. Assignations and affairs, minor misdemeanours and fallings-out. As the show's director had said: *it's a pressure cooker, but if you try turning the heat down sometimes the production suffers.* And in the end, it was all about the show, its run sold out weeks before opening.

'Quite the drama,' Siobhan Clarke said, reading over Rebus's shoulder. She was carrying a cardboard coffee-cup and a leather satchel. 'Maxtone not in yet?'

'Think I'd be here if he was?'

'Fair point.' She put down her things and started removing her long woollen coat. 'I meant to ask you – what are you doing for Christmas?'

'Probably not going to the panto.'

'I mean the day itself – you know you'd be welcome at mine.'

'Thanks, Siobhan, but I have my own traditions to stick to.'

'Meaning finding a pub that's open? Maybe a meal from the freezer after?'

'I'm old-fashioned that way.'

'I feel bad about us shutting down *Cinderella*.'

'We're not the villains here, remember that. Though sometimes all Doug Maxtone lacks is a moustache to twirl.' Rebus looked at his watch. 'Shouldn't have bothered taking your coat off.'

'Is the heating playing up or something?'

Rebus shook his head. 'But we're going out again.'

'We are? Why's that?'

'Because Edwin Oakes is a creature of habit,' he said, rising to his feet.

They decided on Rebus's car so Clarke could continue drinking her coffee, but as they turned out of the car park, they were blocked by a man, his arms outstretched. He wore a flapping coat and was wide-eyed and unshaven.

'Isn't that one of our Ugly Sisters?' Clarke asked.

Rebus was already out of the car. 'Mr Gloag, isn't it?' he was saying.

'I know what he told you and it's not true! Not one word of it!' There were flecks of foam at the corners of the actor's mouth.

'Just calm down.' Rebus held up the palms of both hands. 'I know everyone's a bit on edge …'

'He told you I'd slept with Celia, didn't he?'

'Are we talking about your colleague Davie Clegg?' Clarke inquired.

'Last time I work with that wretched piece of …' Gloag looked at his hands, willing them to stop shaking. 'He told you about *Earnest?* It's true, I was in the same play as her, but nothing ever happened. I mean … she flirted a bit. You know – all touchy-feely, and maybe I picked up the signals wrong.'

'You'd have been accommodating?' Rebus guessed.

'But if you think that was going to make me jealous of Ed …'

'You knew about them though?' Clarke probed.

'We all *knew.*'

'But it didn't make you angry?' Rebus asked. 'The same anger you're feeling right now?'

'I'm not angry.' Gloag tried to laugh. 'I just can't believe Davie would have said anything.'

'Rest easy then, Mr Gloag – Davie Clegg didn't tell tales.'

Gloag looked as if he'd been hit. 'Wh-what?'

'He's been winding you up, sir,' Rebus confirmed. 'Telling you he did something he didn't.'

Colour rose to Gloag's cheeks. 'That does it!' he spat. 'If he thinks we're working together again, he can bloody well whistle. That's our divorce papers right there!' He span away, hurtling down the pavement.

'Think we should warn Clegg?' Clarke asked, getting back into the car.

'We need to be elsewhere.' Rebus started the car. After a minute of silence, he asked about Oakes.

'Shares a flat in the Grassmarket with Buttons. Though apparently they don't see much of one another.'

'Because Buttons is shacked up with the Wicked Stepmother?'

'Reading between the lines, yes. Bit awkward, with both flatmates carrying on their little liaisons. Oakes's actual home is in Glasgow but he hardly gets back there during the season.'

'Officers have been to both?'

'Camped outside through the night,' Clarke confirmed.

'We've also interviewed Prince Charming's ex-wife plus our esteemed director's partner – he's gay, by the way. And the substance abuse?' She shook her head. 'I don't buy it – he's just naturally hyper.' She peered from the window. 'Where are we headed?'

'The Meadows.'

'Is this your security guy again?'

'He's like a priest – they all tell him their story at some point.'

'Stagehands mostly knew about Oakes and Celia Jagger.' Clarke took another sip from her cup. 'I mean, they knew or they'd had an inkling. Seems she had a bit of history in that department – every production she was in, she managed an affair with someone in the cast. Doesn't seem to matter that she was old enough to be Oakes's mother – actually, maybe even his grandmother.'

'But she decides he's not the one – maybe has her eye on someone else. So he burns the photo and then whacks her over the head.'

'It's a fairly classic set-up.'

'You may be wiser than you know.'

'How so?'

'The relevant phrase is "set up".'

She stared at him as he stopped the car kerbside. They were on Melville Drive. The Meadows was an expanse of playing fields criss-crossed by paths. A lot of students used it as a route to the university. In summer, they would host barbecues and games of Frisbee, but there was an icy wind today and the few pedestrians were well wrapped up.

'I wish you'd tell me what's in that head of yours,' Clarke complained. Rebus just winked and got out of the car. She followed him to where he had come to a halt, next to a line of trees. There was a circuit of bare earth, the grass worn away by a generation of joggers. Two young women passed them, managing to hold a conversation while they ran. From the opposite direction came an older man, headphones on, steam rising from his singlet. And then, fifty yards or so back, a figure that seemed out of place. He was dressed in cream chinos and a zip-up jacket, below which was an open-necked shirt. Yes, because Edwin Oakes hadn't felt able to return to his digs or to the theatre. He was wearing the same outfit as when he'd walked out of the police station. And Rebus guessed he hadn't slept either. Despite which, he had come for his morning run.

A creature of habit, just as Willie Mearns had said.

Rebus stepped on to the trail, blocking him. Oakes came to a stop, leaning forward to catch his breath.

'Morning, Mr Oakes,' Rebus said.

'You're the police?' Oakes guessed.

'We need you at St Leonard's, sir.'

Oakes straightened his back. 'I didn't do anything.'

'You ran away,' Clarke corrected him.

'I knew you'd think …' He broke off and shook his head. 'I just needed some time.'

'To come up with a story?'

'To *grieve*.' His eyes bored into Clarke's. 'I loved her. I mean, I knew her reputation and everything – once the show ended, we'd be history. But all the same …'

'She gave you a photo,' Rebus said. 'We found it in the waste-bin in her dressing-room.'

Oakes frowned. 'Nobody knew about that.'

'You're saying you didn't set light to it?' Clarke demanded.

'I kept it in a drawer in my own dressing-room, tucked away where it wouldn't be seen.'

'Somebody found it,' Rebus stated. He half-turned towards Clarke. 'No raised voices from behind Celia Jagger's door – someone from the crew would have heard an argument, they all seem to have pretty good ears.'

'I could never have hurt her,' Oakes was saying. 'Never in a million years.'

'Yet you did a runner.'

'I knew you'd find out about us – either that or I'd have to tell you.' Oakes rubbed at his hair. 'I've a girlfriend – sort of – back in Glasgow. Someone I'm fond of. She's got a daughter who dotes on me. It was the look on her face I couldn't stand, finding out I'd cheated on her mum ...'

'You need to come back with us,' Rebus said quietly. 'We know you didn't do anything. Talking to us means taking us a step closer to finding whoever did.'

Oakes nodded slowly. Clarke's eyes were on Rebus. He knew what she was thinking: *How can we be sure?* As they escorted Oakes to the waiting car, she asked the actor when he had last seen the photo.

'A few days back. Maybe longer than that. It actually hurt me a little.'

'Why was that?'

'It's the sort of thing you hand to a fan at the stage door. I mean, the message was personal but not *that* personal. And that was actually the real message – none of this means anything except in the moment. Soon as the production ends, we go our separate ways.' Oakes angled his head back, as if to stop the tears coming.

Just as well someone usually writes your lines for you, Rebus thought, before inquiring whether Oakes had ever walked into his dressing room and found someone from the cast or crew there.

'All the time – it's an open house. I've usually got chocolate biscuits or cans of cola. Jamie's a demon for the sugar.'

'Jamie meaning Buttons?'

Oakes nodded. 'And John's always wandering in with

some sure-fire bet he wants to share. They're like family …' His face darkened. 'It can't be any of them. There must be someone else.'

'Maybe so, Mr Oakes. Maybe so.' Rebus pulled a slip of paper from his pocket and handed it across for Siobhan Clarke to take.

'See if you can track down this guy,' he said. 'He's the one we probably need to talk to now.'

She read the name. 'Howard Corbyn? Who the hell is Howard Corbyn?'

'You're a detective,' Rebus told her. 'You'll work it out.'

They installed Oakes in the back of the car. But before getting in, Clarke grabbed Rebus by the arm.

'Maxtone needs to know you're the one who did this.' She gestured towards the actor.

'I don't mind you grabbing the good reviews, Siobhan.' She narrowed her eyes. 'It's not over, is it? There's another act coming?'

Rebus nodded towards the slip of paper. 'Depends what comes from that,' he said, making his way round to the driver's seat.

Rebus stood alone on the stage of the Theatre Royal. A stage-hand had raised the curtain and put on a few lights. The scene was still set for the opening of the panto's second half – the kitchen of Baron Hardup's castle. Close up, the set and props looked tired, paint fading or flaking, edges chipped – not unlike the building itself. He knew that council officials had ordered expensive modifications (yet to be carried out). The roof needed repairs and the carpets were fraying or threadbare.

None of which would have mattered to each day's audience, primed with sugary snacks and drinks, pockets emptied in the purchase of glo-sticks, magic wands and glossy programmes. Each year's twelve-week panto run just about made up for nine months of loss-making. The box office next door had been handing out refunds when Rebus arrived. The apology taped over the poster for *Cinderella* said that the show had been cancelled "until further notice".

'Is there any news?' Alan Yates asked, coming on to the stage from the wings.

'Isn't that bad luck?' Rebus said. Yates looked confused. 'You entered stage left. Lighting director told me the show was cursed from the moment Celia Jagger made the mistake of entering stage left during the first rehearsal. Stage left is for villains. Goes back to the medieval mysteries or something.'

Yates forced a smile. 'Stage left is hell, stage right heaven – I know the story, but it's only actors who are superstitious that way. Theatre owners live in the real world – we're even allowed to say the word Macbeth, as long as none of the cast is in earshot...'

'You might have just jinxed yourself then, Mr Yates. You asked if there's news and there is – we've got Russell Gloag in a cell at St Leonard's.'

'Russell?' Yates sounded disbelieving.

'He gave Davie Clegg a bit of a battering – so it looks like you've lost your Ugly Sisters, too. The real world you live in isn't doing you any favours, eh?' Rebus paused. 'Bit of a blow to your ego, I dare say, when your Fairy God-mother decided on Edwin Oakes.'

Yates's face creased. 'I'm not sure I follow.'

'She played here seven years ago in *The Mousetrap*. Then again three years later in an Oscar Wilde play ...'

'Yes?'

'And both times you enjoyed what Wilde might have called "a dalliance".'

Yates's face was colouring. 'We most certainly did not.'

'Oh yes, you did. Crew at the time knew it. *Everyone* knew it. So you reckoned it would be the same again this year. Must have hurt your pride to be rebuffed.' Rebus took a step closer. 'In the lane outside the stage door – the lane covered by CCTV. Willie Mearns saw you. Trying for a clinch, being pushed away. A pointed finger, a slap, a few angry words.'

'This is preposterous.' Yates made to lean against the

table, but it creaked, reminding him that it was not solid. 'You're suggesting I killed Celia because she was seeing Oakes?'

'Not at all.' Rebus paused again. 'You killed her out of simple greed, more than anything. You're like Baron Hardup with a castle that's going to ruin you.' Rebus gestured to the set. 'Just the single solitary panto run each year keeping the creditors from your door. But all the renovations and improvements that need to be made … It'd be years before you saw any return. If the panto could be stopped from spinning gold, you'd have the perfect excuse to sell the place off – no one would blame you or paint you as the villain. That's why you started talking to Howard Corbyn.'

'Who?'

'Howard Corbyn,' Rebus repeated.

'I've never heard of him.'

'Is that right? Well, he's a property developer.' Rebus turned towards the auditorium and raised his voice a little. 'Aren't you, Mr Corbyn?'

He was seated in the front row of the Grand Circle, Siobhan Clarke next to him, the pair of them just about visible beyond the stage lighting. Corbyn nodded and waved, and Alan Yates swallowed a gulp. Perspiration made his face gleam.

'Willie Mearns watched the pair of you,' Rebus went

on, turning towards Yates again. 'Three visits when you knew the theatre would be empty. A handshake in the lane at the end of the third. Flats, commercial use, maybe a super-pub – Mr Corbyn wasn't sure what he would do with the place, but he wanted it if the price was right. You just had to shut down *Cinderella*. *A* real-life tragedy would do the trick. You could get back at Celia Jagger for her snub, and maybe even put her lover in the frame – all you had to do was take that photo from his dressing-room and place it in hers – just singed enough to look the part. You think we can't lift fingerprints from a half-burned picture, Mr Yates? You'd be surprised what we can do these days with anything less than cinders.'

Yates was looking at the floor, as if willing it to reveal an escape route.

'No disappearing act for you,' Rebus warned him. 'But you might want to take one last good look around. Because you know where your reputation's going to be from now on?'

'Where?' Yates couldn't help asking, his voice cracking.

Instead of answering, Rebus looked up to where Siobhan Clarke was sitting.

'Behind you!' she called down.

'Behind you,' Rebus repeated quietly, leading Alan Yates from the stage.

Death on the Air

Ngaio Marsh

On the 25th of December at 7:30 a.m. Mr Septimus Tonks was found dead beside his wireless set.

It was Emily Parks, an under-housemaid, who discovered him. She butted open the door and entered, carrying mop, duster, and carpet-sweeper. At that precise moment she was greatly startled by a voice that spoke out of the darkness.

'Good morning, everybody,' said the voice in superbly inflected syllables, 'and a Merry Christmas!'

Emily yelped, but not loudly, as she immediately realised what had happened. Mr Tonks had omitted to turn off his wireless before going to bed. She drew back the curtains, revealing a kind of pale murk which was a London Christmas dawn, switched on the light, and saw Septimus.

He was seated in front of the radio. It was a small but expensive set, specially built for him. Septimus sat in an armchair, his back to Emily, his body tilted towards the radio.

His hands, the fingers curiously bunched, were on the ledge of the cabinet under the tuning and volume knobs. His chest rested against the shelf below and his head leaned on the front panel.

He looked rather as though he was listening intently to the interior secrets of the wireless. His head was bent so that Emily could see his bald top with its trail of oiled hairs. He did not move.

'Beg pardon, sir,' gasped Emily. She was again greatly startled. Mr Tonks's enthusiasm for radio had never before induced him to tune in at seven-thirty in the morning.

'Special Christmas service,' the cultured voice was saying. Mr Tonks sat very still. Emily, in common with the other servants, was terrified of her master. She did not know whether to go or to stay. She gazed wildly at Septimus and realised that he wore a dinner-jacket. The room was now filled with the clamour of pealing bells.

Emily opened her mouth as wide as it would go and screamed and screamed and screamed …

Chase, the butler, was the first to arrive. He was a pale, flabby man but authoritative. He said: 'What's the meaning of this outrage?' and then saw Septimus. He went to the armchair, bent down, and looked into his master's face.

He did not lose his head, but said in a loud voice: 'My Gawd!' And then to Emily: 'Shut your face.' By this vulgarism he betrayed his agitation. He seized Emily by the shoulders and thrust her towards the door, where they were met by Mr Hislop, the secretary, in his dressing-gown. Mr Hislop said: 'Good heavens, Chase, what is the meaning – ' and then his voice too was drowned in the clamour of bells and renewed screams.

Chase put his fat white hand over Emily's mouth.

'In the study if you please, sir. An accident. Go to your room, will you, and stop that noise or I'll give you something to make you.' This to Emily, who bolted down the hall, where she was received by the rest of the staff who had congregated there.

Chase returned to the study with Mr Hislop and locked the door. They both looked down at the body of Septimus Tonks. The secretary was the first to speak.

'But – but – he's dead,' said little Mr Hislop.

'I suppose there can't be any doubt,' whispered Chase.

'Look at the face. Any doubt! My God!'

Mr Hislop put out a delicate hand towards the bent head and then drew it back. Chase, less fastidious, touched one of the hard wrists, gripped, and then lifted it. The body at once tipped backwards as if it was made of wood. One of the hands knocked against the butler's face. He sprang back with an oath.

There lay Septimus, his knees and his hands in the air, his terrible face turned up to the light. Chase pointed to the right hand. Two fingers and the thumb were slightly blackened.

Ding, dong, dang, ding.

'For God's sake stop those bells,' cried Mr Hislop. Chase turned off the wall switch. Into the sudden silence came the sound of the door-handle being rattled and Guy Tonks's voice on the other side.

'Hislop! Mr Hislop! Chase! What's the matter?'

'Just a moment, Mr Guy.' Chase looked at the secretary. 'You go, sir.'

So it was left to Mr Hislop to break the news to the family. They listened to his stammering revelation in stupefied silence. It was not until Guy, the eldest of the three children, stood in the study that any practical suggestion was made.

'What has killed him?' asked Guy.

'It's extraordinary,' burbled Hislop. 'Extraordinary. He looks as if he'd been – '

'Galvanised,' said Guy.

'We ought to send for a doctor,' suggested Hislop timidly.

'Of course. Will you, Mr Hislop? Dr Meadows.'

Hislop went to the telephone and Guy returned to his family. Dr Meadows lived on the other side of the square and arrived in five minutes. He examined the body without moving it. He questioned Chase and Hislop. Chase was very voluble about the burns on the hand. He uttered the word 'electrocution' over and over again.

'I had a cousin, sir, that was struck by lightning. As soon as I saw the hand – '

'Yes, yes,' said Dr Meadows. 'So you said. I can see the burns for myself.'

'Electrocution,' repeated Chase. 'There'll have to be an inquest.'

Dr Meadows snapped at him, summoned Emily, and then saw the rest of the family – Guy, Arthur, Phillipa, and their mother. They were clustered round a cold grate in the drawing-room. Phillipa was on her knees, trying to light the fire.

'What was it?' asked Arthur as soon as the doctor came in.

'Looks like electric shock. Guy, I'll have a word with you if you please. Phillipa, look after your mother, there's a good child. Coffee with a dash of brandy. Where are those damn maids? Come on, Guy.'

Alone with Guy, he said they'd have to send for the police.

'The police!' Guy's dark face turned very pale. 'Why? What's it got to do with them?'

'Nothing, as like as not, but they'll have to be notified.

147

I can't give a certificate as things are. If it's electrocution, how did it happen?'

'But the police!' said Guy. 'That's simply ghastly. Dr Meadows, for God's sake couldn't you?'

'No,' said Dr Meadows, 'I couldn't. Sorry, Guy, but there it is.'

'But can't we wait a moment? Look at him again. You haven't examined him properly.'

'I don't want to move him, that's why. Pull yourself together, boy. Look here. I've got a pal in the CID – Alleyn. He's a gentleman and all that. He'll curse me like a fury, but he'll come if he's in London, and he'll make things easier for you. Go back to your mother. I'll ring Alleyn up.'

That was how it came about that Chief Detective-Inspector Roderick Alleyn spent his Christmas Day in harness. As a matter of fact he was on duty, and as he pointed out to Dr Meadows, would have had to turn out and visit his miserable Tonkses in any case. When he did arrive it was with his usual air of remote courtesy. He was accompanied by a tall, thick-set officer – Inspector Fox – and by the divisional police-surgeon. Dr Meadows took them into the study. Alleyn, in his turn, looked at the horror that had been Septimus.

'Was he like this when he was found?'

'No. I understand he was leaning forward with his hands

on the ledge of the cabinet. He must have slumped forward and been propped up by the chair arms and the cabinet.'

'Who moved him?'

'Chase, the butler. He said he only meant to raise the arm. *Rigor* is well established.'

Alleyn put his hand behind the rigid neck and pushed. The body fell forward into its original position.

'There you are, Curtis,' said Alleyn to the divisional surgeon. He turned to Fox. 'Get the camera man, will you, Fox?'

The photographer took four shots and departed. Alleyn marked the position of the hands and feet with chalk, made a careful plan of the room and turned to the doctors.

'Is it electrocution, do you think?'

'Looks like it,' said Curtis. 'Have to be a PM, of course.'

'Of course. Still, look at the hands. Burns. Thumb and two fingers bunched together and exactly the distance between the two knobs apart. He'd been tuning his hurdy-gurdy.'

'By gum,' said Inspector Fox, speaking for the first time.

'D'you mean he got a lethal shock from his radio?' asked Dr Meadows.

'I don't know. I merely conclude he had his hands on the knobs when he died.'

'It was still going when the housemaid found him.

Chase turned it off and got no shock.'

'Yours, partner,' said Alleyn, turning to Fox. Fox stooped down to the wall switch.

'Careful,' said Alleyn.

'I've got rubber soles,' said Fox, and switched it on. The radio hummed, gathered volume, and found itself.

'No-o-el, No-o-el,' it roared. Fox cut it off and pulled out the wall plug.

'I'd like to have a look inside this set,' he said.

'So you shall, old boy, so you shall,' rejoined Alleyn. 'Before you begin, I think we'd better move the body. Will you see to that, Meadows? Fox, get Bailey, will you? He's out in the car.'

Curtis, Hislop, and Meadows carried Septimus Tonks into a spare downstairs room. It was a difficult and horrible business with that contorted body. Dr Meadows came back alone, mopping his brow, to find Detective-Sergeant Bailey, a fingerprint expert, at work on the wireless cabinet.

'What's all this?' asked Dr Meadows. 'Do you want to find out if he'd been fooling round with the innards?'

'He,' said Alleyn, 'or – somebody else.'

'Umph!' Dr Meadows looked at the Inspector. 'You agree with me, it seems. Do you suspect – ?'

'Suspect? I'm the least suspicious man alive. I'm merely being tidy. Well, Bailey?'

'I've got a good one off the chair arm. That'll be the deceased's, won't it, sir?'

'No doubt. We'll check up later. What about the wireless?'

Fox, wearing a glove, pulled off the knob of the volume control.

'Seems to be OK,' said Bailey. 'It's a sweet bit of work. Not too bad at all, sir.' He turned his torch into the back of the radio, undid a couple of screws underneath the set, lifted out the works.

'What's the little hole for?' asked Alleyn.

'What's that, sir?' said Fox.

'There's a hole bored through the panel above the knob. About an eighth of an inch in diameter. The rim of the knob hides it. One might easily miss it. Move your torch, Bailey. Yes. There, do you see?'

Fox bent down and uttered a bass growl. A fine needle of light came through the front of the radio.

'That's peculiar, sir,' said Bailey from the other side. 'I don't get the idea at all.'

Alleyn pulled out the tuning knob.

'There's another one there,' he murmured. 'Yes. Nice clean little holes. Newly bored. Unusual, I take it?'

'Unusual's the word, sir,' said Fox.

'Run away, Meadows,' said Alleyn.

'Why the devil?' asked Dr Meadows indignantly. 'What

are you driving at? Why shouldn't I be here?'

'You ought to be with the sorrowing relatives. Where's your corpseside manner?'

'I've settled them. What are you up to?'

'Who's being suspicious now?' asked Alleyn mildly. 'You may stay for a moment. Tell me about the Tonkses. Who are they? What are they? What sort of a man was Septimus?'

'If you must know, he was a damned unpleasant sort of a man.'

'Tell me about him.'

Dr Meadows sat down and lit a cigarette.

'He was a self-made bloke,' he said, 'as hard as nails and – well, coarse rather than vulgar.'

'Like Dr Johnson perhaps?'

'Not in the least. Don't interrupt. I've known him for twenty-five years. His wife was a neighbour of ours in Dorset. Isabel Foreston. I brought the children into this vale of tears and, by jove, in many ways it's been one for them. It's an extraordinary household. For the last ten years Isabel's condition has been the sort that sends these psycho-jokers dizzy with rapture. I'm only an out-of-date GP, and I'd just say she is in an advanced stage of hysterical neurosis. Frightened into fits of her husband.'

'I can't understand these holes,' grumbled Fox to Bailey.

'Go on, Meadows,' said Alleyn.

'I tackled Sep about her eighteen months ago. Told him the trouble was in her mind. He eyed me with a sort of grin on his face and said: "I'm surprised to learn that my wife has enough mentality to – " But look here, Alleyn, I can't talk about my patients like this. What the devil am I thinking about.'

'You know perfectly well it'll go no further unless – '

'Unless what?'

'Unless it has to. Do go on.'

But Dr Meadows hurriedly withdrew behind his professional rectitude. All he would say was that Mr Tonks had suffered from high blood pressure and a weak heart, that Guy was in his father's city office, that Arthur had wanted to study art and had been told to read for law, and that Phillipa wanted to go on to the stage and had been told to do nothing of the sort.

'Bullied his children,' commented Alleyn.

'Find out for yourself. I'm off.' Dr Meadows got as far as the door and came back.

'Look here,' he said, 'I'll tell you one thing. There was a row here last night. I'd asked Hislop, who's a sensible little beggar, to let me know if anything happened to upset Mrs Sep. Upset her badly, you know. To be indiscreet again, I said he'd better let me know if Sep cut up rough, because Isabel and the young had had about as much of that as they could stand. He was drinking pretty heavily. Hislop rang me up at ten-twenty last night to say there'd been a hell of a row; Sep bullying Phips – Phillipa, you know; always call her Phips – in her room. He said Isabel – Mrs Sep – had gone to bed. I'd had a big day and I didn't want to turn out. I told him to ring again in half an hour if things hadn't quieted down. I told him to keep out of Sep's way and stay in his own room, which is next to Phips's, and see if she was all right when Sep cleared out. Hislop was involved. I won't tell you how. The servants were all out. I said that if I didn't hear from him in half an hour I'd ring again and if there was no answer I'd know they were all in bed and quiet. I did ring, got no answer, and went to bed myself. That's all. I'm off. Curtis knows where to find me. You'll want me for the inquest, I suppose. Goodbye.'

When he had gone Alleyn embarked on a systematic prowl round the room. Fox and Bailey were still deeply engrossed with the wireless.

'I don't see how the gentleman could have got a bump-off from the instrument,' grumbled Fox. 'These control knobs are quite in order. Everything's as it should be. Look here, sir.'

He turned on the wall switch and tuned in. There was a prolonged humming.

'... concludes the programme of Christmas carols,' said the radio.

'A very nice tone,' said Fox approvingly.

'Here's something, sir,' announced Bailey suddenly.

'Found the sawdust, have you?' said Alleyn.

'Got it in one,' said the startled Bailey.

Alleyn peered into the instrument, using the torch. He scooped up two tiny traces of sawdust from under the holes.

'Vantage number one,' said Alleyn. He bent down to the wall plug. 'Hullo! A two-way adapter. Serves the radio and the radiator. Thought they were illegal. This is a rum business. Let's have another look at those knobs.'

He had his look. They were the usual wireless fitments, Bakelite knobs fitting snugly to the steel shafts that projected from the front panel.

'As you say,' he murmured, 'quite in order. Wait a bit.' He produced a pocket lens and squinted at one of the shafts. 'Ye-es. Do they ever wrap blotting-paper round these objects, Fox?'

'Blotting-paper!' ejaculated Fox. 'They do not.'

Alleyn scraped at both the shafts with his penknife, holding an envelope underneath. He rose, groaning, and crossed to the desk. 'A corner torn off the bottom bit of blotch,' he said presently. 'No prints on the wireless, I think you said, Bailey?'

'That's right,' agreed Bailey morosely.

'There'll be none, or too many, on the blotter, but try,

Bailey, try,' said Alleyn. He wandered about the room, his eyes on the floor; got as far as the window and stopped.

'Fox!' he said. 'A clue. A very palpable clue.'

'What is it?' asked Fox.

'The odd wisp of blotting-paper, no less.' Alleyn's gaze travelled up the side of the window curtain. 'Can I believe my eyes?'

He got a chair, stood on the seat, and with his gloved hand pulled the buttons from the ends of the curtain-rod.

'Look at this.' He turned to the radio, detached the control knobs, and laid them beside the ones he had removed from the curtain-rod.

Ten minutes later Inspector Fox knocked on the drawing-room door and was admitted by Guy Tonks. Phillipa had got the fire going and the family was gathered round it. They looked as though they had not moved or spoken to one another for a long time.

It was Phillipa who spoke first to Fox. 'Do you want one of us?'

'If you please, miss,' said Fox. 'Inspector Alleyn would like to see Mr Guy Tonks for a moment, if convenient.'

'I'll come,' said Guy, and led the way to the study. At the door he paused. 'Is he – my father – still – ?'

'No, no, sir,' said Fox comfortably. 'It's all ship-shape in there again.'

With a lift of his chin Guy opened the door and went

in, followed by Fox. Alleyn was alone, seated at the desk. He rose to his feet.

'You want to speak to me?' asked Guy.

'Yes, if I may. This has all been a great shock to you, of course. Won't you sit down?'

Guy sat in the chair farthest away from the radio.

'What killed my father? Was it a stroke?'

'The doctors are not quite certain. There will have to be a post-mortem.'

'Good God! And an inquest?'

'I'm afraid so.'

'Horrible!' said Guy violently. 'What do you think was the matter? Why the devil do these quacks have to be so mysterious? What killed him?'

'They think an electric shock.'

'How did it happen?'

'We don't know. It looks as if he got it from the wireless.'

'Surely that's impossible. I thought they were fool-proof.'

'I believe they are, if left to themselves.'

For a second undoubtedly Guy was startled. Then a look of relief came into his eyes. He seemed to relax all over.

'Of course,' he said, 'he was always monkeying about with it. What had he done?'

'Nothing.'

'But you said – if it killed him he must have done something to it.'

'If anyone interfered with the set it was put right afterwards.'

Guy's lips parted but he did not speak. He had gone very white.

'So you see,' said Alleyn, 'your father could not have done anything.'

'Then it was not the radio that killed him.'

'That we hope will be determined by the post-mortem.'

'I don't know anything about wireless,' said Guy suddenly. 'I don't understand. This doesn't seem to make sense. Nobody ever touched the thing except my father. He was most particular about it. Nobody went near the wireless.'

'I see. He was an enthusiast?'

'Yes, it was his only enthusiasm except – except his business.'

'One of my men is a bit of an expert,' Alleyn said. 'He says this is a remarkably good set. You are not an expert, you say. Is there anyone in the house who is?'

'My young brother was interested at one time. He's given it up. My father wouldn't allow another radio in the house.'

'Perhaps he may be able to suggest something.'

'But if the thing's all right now –'

'We've got to explore every possibility.'

'You speak as if – as – if – '

'I speak as I am bound to speak before there has been an inquest,' said Alleyn. 'Had anyone a grudge against your father, Mr Tonks?'

Up went Guy's chin again. He looked Alleyn squarely in the eyes.

'Almost everyone who knew him,' said Guy.

'Is that an exaggeration?'

'No. You think he was murdered, don't you?'

Alleyn suddenly pointed to the desk beside him.

'Have you ever seen those before?' he asked abruptly. Guy stared at two black knobs that lay side by side on an ashtray.

'Those?' he said. 'No. What are they?'

'I believe they are the agents of your father's death.'

The study door opened and Arthur Tonks came in.

'Guy,' he said, 'what's happening? We can't stay cooped up together all day. I can't stand it. For God's sake what happened to him?'

'They think those things killed him,' said Guy.

'Those?' For a split second Arthur's glance slewed to the curtain-rods. Then, with a characteristic flicker of his eyelids, he looked away again.

'What do you mean?' he asked Alleyn.

'Will you try one of those knobs on the shaft of the volume control?'

'But,' said Arthur, 'they're metal.'

'It's disconnected,' said Alleyn.

Arthur picked one of the knobs from the tray, turned to the radio, and fitted the knob over one of the exposed shafts.

'It's too loose,' he said quickly, 'it would fall off.'

'Not if it was packed – with blotting-paper, for instance.'

'Where did you find these things?' demanded Arthur.

'I think you recognised them, didn't you? I saw you glance at the curtain-rod.'

'Of course I recognised them. I did a portrait of Phillipa against those curtains when – he – was away last year. I've painted the damn things.'

'Look here,' interrupted Guy, 'exactly what are you driving at, Mr Alleyn? If you mean to suggest that my brother – '

'I!' cried Arthur. 'What's it got to do with me? Why should you suppose – '

'I found traces of blotting-paper on the shafts and inside the metal knobs,' said Alleyn. 'It suggested a substitution of the metal knobs for the Bakelite ones. It is remarkable, don't you think, that they should so closely resemble one another? If you examine them, of course, you find they are not identical. Still, the difference is scarcely perceptible.'

Arthur did not answer this. He was still looking at the wireless.

'I've always wanted to have a look at this set,' he said surprisingly.

'You are free to do so now,' said Alleyn politely. 'We have finished with it for the time being.'

'Look here,' said Arthur suddenly, 'suppose metal knobs were substituted for Bakelite ones, it couldn't kill him. He wouldn't get a shock at all. Both the controls are grounded.'

'Have you noticed those very small holes drilled through the panel?' asked Alleyn. 'Should they be there, do you think?'

Arthur peered at the little steel shafts. 'By God, he's right, Guy,' he said. 'That's how it was done.'

'Inspector Fox,' said Alleyn, 'tells me those holes could be used for conducting wires and that a lead could be taken from the – the transformer, is it? – to one of the knobs.'

'And the other connected to earth,' said Fox. 'It's a job for an expert. He could get three hundred volts or so that way.'

'That's not good enough,' said Arthur quickly; 'there wouldn't be enough current to do any damage – only a few hundredths of an amp.'

'I'm not an expert,' said Alleyn, 'but I'm sure you're right. Why were the holes drilled then? Do you imagine someone wanted to play a practical joke on your father?'

'A practical joke? On *him*?' Arthur gave an unpleasant screech of laughter. 'Do you hear that, Guy?'

'Shut up,' said Guy. 'After all, he is dead.'

'It seems almost too good to be true, doesn't it?'

'Don't be a bloody fool, Arthur. Pull yourself together. Can't you see what this means? They think he's been murdered.'

'Murdered! They're wrong. None of us had the nerve for that, Mr Inspector. Look at me. My hands are so shaky they told me I'd never be able to paint. That dates from when I was a kid and he shut me up in the cellars for a night. Look at me. Look at Guy. He's not so vulnerable, but he caved in like the rest of us. We were conditioned to surrender. Do you know — '

'Wait a moment,' said Alleyn quietly. 'Your brother is quite right, you know. You'd better think before you speak. This may be a case of homicide.'

'Thank you, sir,' said Guy quickly. 'That's extraordinarily decent of you. Arthur's a bit above himself. It's a shock.'

'The relief, you mean,' said Arthur. 'Don't be such an ass. I didn't kill him and they'll find it out soon enough. Nobody killed him. There must be some explanation.'

'I suggest that you listen to me,' said Alleyn. 'I'm going to put several questions to both of you. You need not answer them, but it will be more sensible to do so. I understand no one but your father touched this radio. Did any of you ever come into this room while it was in use?'

'Not unless he wanted to vary the programme with a little bullying,' said Arthur.

Alleyn turned to Guy, who was glaring at his brother.

'I want to know exactly what happened in this house last night. As far as the doctors can tell us, your father died not less than three and not more than eight hours before he was found. We must try to fix the time as accurately as possible.'

'I saw him at about a quarter to nine,' began Guy slowly. 'I was going out to a supper-party at the Savoy and had come downstairs. He was crossing the hall from the drawing-room to his room.'

'Did you see him after a quarter to nine, Mr Arthur?'

'No. I heard him, though. He was working in here with Hislop. Hislop had asked to go away for Christmas. Quite enough. My father discovered some urgent correspondence. Really, Guy, you know, he was pathological. I'm sure Dr Meadows thinks so.'

'When did you hear him?' asked Alleyn.

'Some time after Guy had gone. I was working on a drawing in my room upstairs. It's above his. I heard him bawling at little Hislop. It must have been before ten o'clock, because I went out to a studio party at ten. I heard him bawling as I crossed the hall.'

'And when,' said Alleyn, 'did you both return?'

'I came home at about twenty past twelve,' said Guy immediately. 'I can fix the time because we had gone on to Chez Carlo, and they had a midnight stunt there. We left immediately afterwards. I came home in a taxi. The radio was on full blast.'

'You heard no voices?'

'None. Just the wireless.'

'And you, Mr Arthur?'

'Lord knows when I got in. After one. The house was in darkness. Not a sound.'

'You had your own key?'

'Yes,' said Guy. 'Each of us has one. They're always left on a hook in the lobby. When I came in I noticed Arthur's was gone.'

'What about the others? How did you know it was his?'

'Mother hasn't got one and Phips lost hers weeks ago. Anyway, I knew they were staying in and that it must be Arthur who was out.'

'Thank you,' said Arthur ironically.

'You didn't look in the study when you came in?' Alleyn asked him.

'Good Lord, no,' said Arthur as if the suggestion was fantastic. 'I say,' he said suddenly, 'I suppose he was sitting here – dead. That's a queer thought.' He laughed nervously. 'Just sitting here, behind the door in the dark.'

'How do you know it was in the dark?'

'What d'you mean? Of course it was. There was no light under the door.'

'I see. Now do you two mind joining your mother again? Perhaps your sister will be kind enough to come in here for a moment. Fox, ask her, will you?'

Fox returned to the drawing-room with Guy and Arthur and remained there, blandly unconscious of any embarrassment his presence might cause the Tonkses. Bailey was already there, ostensibly examining the electric points.

Phillipa went to the study at once. Her first remark was characteristic. 'Can I be of any help?' asked Phillipa.

'It's extremely nice of you to put it like that,' said Alleyn. 'I don't want to worry you for long. I'm sure this discovery has been a shock to you.'

'Probably,' said Phillipa. Alleyn glanced quickly at her. 'I mean,' she explained, 'that I suppose I must be shocked but I can't feel anything much. I just want to get it all over as soon as possible. And then think. Please tell me what has happened.'

Alleyn told her they believed her father had been electrocuted and that the circumstances were unusual and puzzling. He said nothing to suggest that the police suspected murder.

'I don't think I'll be much help,' said Phillipa, 'but go ahead.'

'I want to try to discover who was the last person to see your father or speak to him.'

'I should think very likely I was,' said Phillipa composedly. 'I had a row with him before I went to bed.'

'What about?'

'I don't see that it matters.'

Alleyn considered this. When he spoke again it was with deliberation.

'Look here,' he said, 'I think there is very little doubt that your father was killed by an electric shock from his wireless set. As far as I know the circumstances are unique. Radios are normally incapable of giving a lethal shock to anyone. We have examined the cabinet and are inclined to think that its internal arrangements were disturbed last night. Very radically disturbed. Your father may have experimented with it. If anything happened to interrupt or upset him, it is possible that in the excitement of the moment he made some dangerous readjustment.'

'You don't believe that, do you?' asked Phillipa calmly.

'Since you ask me,' said Alleyn, 'no.'

'I see,' said Phillipa; 'you think he was murdered, but you're not sure.' She had gone very white, but she spoke crisply. 'Naturally you want to find out about my row.'

'About everything that happened last evening,' amended Alleyn.

'What happened was this,' said Phillipa; 'I came into the hall some time after ten. I'd heard Arthur go out and had looked at the clock at five past. I ran into my father's secretary, Richard Hislop. He turned aside, but not before I saw … not quickly enough. I blurted out: "You're crying." We looked at each other. I asked him why he stood it. None of the other secretaries could. He said he had to. He's a widower with two children. There have been doctor's bills and things. I needn't tell you about his … about his damnable servitude to my father, nor about the refinements of cruelty he'd had to put up with. I think my father was mad, really mad, I mean. Richard gabbled it all out to me higgledy-piggledy in a sort of horrified whisper. He's been here two years, but I'd never realised until that moment that we … that …' A faint flush came into her cheeks. 'He's such a funny little man. Not at all the sort I've always thought … not good-looking or exciting or anything.'

She stopped, looking bewildered.

'Yes?' said Alleyn.

'Well, you see – I suddenly realised I was in love with him. He realised it too. He said: "Of course, it's quite hopeless, you know. Us, I mean. Laughable, almost.". Then I put my arms round his neck and kissed him. It was very odd, but it seemed quite natural. The point is my father came out of his room into the hall and saw us.'

'That was bad luck,' said Alleyn.

'Yes, it was. My father really seemed delighted. He almost licked his lips. Richard's efficiency had irritated my father for a long time. It was difficult to find excuses for being beastly to him. Now, of course … He ordered Richard to the study and me to my room. He followed me upstairs. Richard tried to come too, but I asked him not to. My father … I needn't tell you what he said. He put the worst possible construction on what he'd seen. He was absolutely foul, screaming at me like a madman. He was insane. Perhaps it was dt's. He drank terribly, you know. I dare say it's silly of me to tell you all this.'

'No,' said Alleyn.

'I can't feel anything at all. Not even relief. The boys are frankly relieved. I can't feel afraid either.' She stared meditatively at Alleyn. 'Innocent people needn't feel afraid, need they?'

'It's an axiom of police investigation,' said Alleyn and wondered if indeed she was innocent.

'It just *can't* be murder,' said Phillipa. 'We were all too much afraid to kill him. I believe he'd win even if you murdered him. He'd hit back somehow.' She put her hands to her eyes. 'I'm all muddled.'

'I think you are more upset than you realise. I'll be as

quick as I can. Your father made this scene in your room. You say he screamed. Did anyone hear him?'

'Yes. Mummy did. She came in.'

'What happened?'

'I said: "Go away, darling, it's all right." I didn't want her to be involved. He nearly killed her with the things he did. Sometimes he'd … we never knew what happened between them. It was all secret, like a door shutting quietly as you walk along a passage.'

'Did she go away?'

'Not at once. He told her he'd found out that Richard and I were lovers. He said … it doesn't matter. I don't want to tell you. She was terrified. He was stabbing at her in some way I couldn't understand. Then, quite suddenly, he told her to go to her own room. She went at once and he followed her. He locked me in. That's the last I saw of him, but I heard him go downstairs later.'

'Were you locked in all night?'

'No. Richard Hislop's room is next to mine. He came up and spoke through the wall to me. He wanted to unlock the door, but I said better not in case – he – came back. Then, much later, Guy came home. As he passed my door I tapped on it. The key was in the lock and he turned it.'

'Did you tell him what had happened?'

'Just that there'd been a row. He only stayed a moment.'

'Can you hear the radio from your room?'

She seemed surprised.

'The wireless? Why, yes. Faintly.'

'Did you hear it after your father returned to the study?'

'I don't remember.'

'Think. While you lay awake all that long time until your brother came home?'

'I'll try. When he came out and found Richard and me, it was not going. They had been working, you see. No, I can't remember hearing it at all unless – wait a moment. Yes. After he had gone back to the study from mother's room I remember there was a loud crash of static. Very loud. Then I think it was quiet for some time. I fancy I heard it again later. Oh, I've remembered something else. After the static my bedside radiator went out. I suppose there was something wrong with the electric supply. That would account for both, wouldn't it? The heater went on again about ten minutes later.'

'And did the radio begin again then, do you think?'

'I don't know. I'm very vague about that. It started again sometime before I went to sleep.'

'Thank you very much indeed. I won't bother you any longer now.'

'All right,' said Phillipa calmly, and went away.

Alleyn sent for Chase and questioned him about the rest

of the staff and about the discovery of the body. Emily was summoned and dealt with. When she departed, awe-struck but complacent, Alleyn turned to the butler.

'Chase,' he said, 'had your master any peculiar habits?'

'Yes, sir.'

'In regard to the wireless?'

'I beg pardon, sir. I thought you meant generally speaking.'

'Well, then, generally speaking.'

'If I may say so, sir, he was a mass of them.'

'How long have you been with him?'

'Two months, sir, and due to leave at the end of this week.'

'Oh. Why are you leaving?'

Chase produced the classic remark of his kind.

'There are some things,' he said, 'that flesh and blood will not stand, sir. One of them's being spoke to like Mr Tonks spoke to his staff.'

'Ah. His peculiar habits, in fact?'

'It's my opinion, sir, he was mad. Stark, staring.'

'With regard to the radio. Did he tinker with it?'

'I can't say I've ever noticed, sir. I believe he knew quite a lot about wireless.'

'When he tuned the thing, had he any particular method? Any characteristic attitude or gesture?'

'I don't think so, sir. I never noticed, and yet I've often

come into the room when he was at it. I can seem to see him now, sir.'

'Yes, yes,' said Alleyn swiftly. 'That's what we want. A clear mental picture. How was it now? Like this?'

In a moment he was across the room and seated in Septimus's chair. He swung round to the cabinet and raised his right hand to the tuning control.

'Like this?'

'No, sir,' said Chase promptly, 'that's not him at all. Both hands it should be.'

'Ah.' Up went Alleyn's left hand to the volume control. 'More like this?'

'Yes, sir,' said Chase slowly. 'But there's something else and I can't recollect what it was. Something he was always doing. It's in the back of my head. You know, sir. Just on the edge of my memory, as you might say.'

'I know.'

'It's a kind – something – to do with irritation,' said Chase slowly.

'Irritation? His?'

'No. It's no good, sir. I can't get it.'

'Perhaps later. Now look here, Chase, what happened to all of you last night? All the servants, I mean.'

'We were all out, sir. It being Christmas Eve. The mistress sent for me yesterday morning. She said we could take the evening off as soon as I had taken in Mr Tonks's grog-tray at nine o'clock. So we went,' ended Chase simply.

'When?'

'The rest of the staff got away about nine. I left at ten past, sir, and returned about eleven-twenty. The others were back then, and all in bed. I went straight to bed myself, sir.'

'You came in by a back door, I suppose?'

'Yes, sir. We've been talking it over. None of us noticed anything unusual.'

'Can you hear the wireless in your part of the house?'

'No, sir.'

'Well,' said Alleyn, looking up from his notes, 'that'll do, thank you.'

Before Chase reached the door, Fox came in.

'Beg pardon, sir,' said Fox, 'I just want to take a look at the *Radio Times* on the desk.'

He bent over the paper, wetted a gigantic thumb, and turned a page.

'That's it, sir,' shouted Chase suddenly. 'That's what I tried to think of. That's what he was always doing.'

'But what?'

'Licking his fingers, sir. It was a habit,' said Chase. 'That's what he always did when he sat down to the radio. I heard Mr Hislop tell the doctor it nearly drove him demented, the way the master couldn't touch a thing without first licking his fingers.'

'Quite so,' said Alleyn. 'In about ten minutes, ask Mr Hislop if he will be good enough to come in for a moment. That will be all, thank you, Chase.'

'Well, sir,' remarked Fox when Chase had gone, 'if that's the case and what I think's right, it'd certainly make matters worse.'

'Good heavens, Fox, what an elaborate remark. What does it mean?'

'If metal knobs were substituted for Bakelite ones and fine wires brought through those holes to make contact, then he'd get a bigger bump if he tuned in with *damp* fingers.'

'Yes. And he always used both hands. Fox!'

'Sir.'

'Approach the Tonkses again. You haven't left them alone, of course?'

'Bailey's in there making out he's interested in the light switches. He's found the main switchboard under the stairs. There's signs of a blown fuse having been fixed recently. In a cupboard underneath there are odd lengths of flex and so on. Same brand as this on the wireless and the heater.'

'Ah, yes. Could the cord from the adapter to the radiator be brought into play?'

'By gum,' said Fox, 'you're right! That's how it was done, Chief. The heavier flex was cut away from the

174

radiator and shoved through. There was a fire, so he wouldn't want the radiator and wouldn't notice.'

'It might have been done that way, certainly, but there's little to prove it. Return to the bereaved Tonkses, my Fox, and ask prettily if any of them remember Septimus's peculiarities when tuning his wireless.'

Fox met little Mr Hislop at the door and left him alone with Alleyn. Phillipa had been right, reflected the Inspector, when she said Richard Hislop was not a noticeable man. He was nondescript. Grey eyes, drab hair; rather pale, rather short, rather insignificant; and yet last night there had flashed up between those two the realisation of love. Romantic but rum, thought Alleyn.

'Do sit down,' he said. 'I want you, if you will, to tell me what happened between you and Mr Tonks last evening.'

'What happened?'

'Yes. You all dined at eight, I understand. Then you and Mr Tonks came in here?'

'Yes.'

'What did you do?'

'He dictated several letters.'

'Anything unusual take place?'

'Oh, no.'

'Why did you quarrel?'

'Quarrel!' The quiet voice jumped a tone. 'We did not quarrel, Mr Alleyn.'

'Perhaps that was the wrong word. What upset you?'

'Phillipa has told you?'

'Yes. She was wise to do so. What was the matter, Mr Hislop?'

'Apart from the ... what she told you ... Mr Tonks was a difficult man to please. I often irritated him. I did so last night.'

'In what way?'

'In almost every way. He shouted at me. I was startled and nervous, clumsy with papers, and making mistakes. I wasn't well. I blundered and then ... I ... I broke down. I have always irritated him. My very mannerisms – '

'Had he no irritating mannerisms, himself?'

'He! My God!'

'What were they?'

'I can't think of anything in particular. It doesn't matter, does it?'

'Anything to do with the wireless, for instance?'

There was a short silence.

'No,' said Hislop.

'Was the radio on in here last night, after dinner?'

'For a little while. Not after – after the incident in the hall. At least, I don't think so. I don't remember.'

'What did you do after Miss Phillipa and her father had gone upstairs?'

'I followed and listened outside the door for a moment.'

He had gone very white and had backed away from the desk.

'And then?'

'I heard someone coming. I remembered Dr Meadows had told me to ring him up if there was one of the scenes. I returned here and rang him up. He told me to go to my room and listen. If things got any worse I was to telephone again. Otherwise I was to stay in my room. It is next to hers.'

'And you did this?' He nodded. 'Could you hear what Mr Tonks said to her?'

'A – a good deal of it.'

'What did you hear?'

'He insulted her. Mrs Tonks was there. I was just thinking of ringing Dr Meadows up again when she and Mr Tonks came out and went along the passage. I stayed in my room.'

'You did not try to speak to Miss Phillipa?'

'We spoke through the wall. She asked me not to ring Dr Meadows, but to stay in my room. In a little while, perhaps it was as much as twenty minutes – I really don't know – I heard him come back and go downstairs. I again spoke to Phillipa. She implored me not to do anything and said that she herself would speak to Dr Meadows in the morning. So I waited a little longer and then went to bed.'

'And to sleep?'

'My God, no!'

'Did you hear the wireless again?'

'Yes. At least I heard static.'

'Are you an expert on wireless?'

'No. I know the ordinary things. Nothing much.'

'How did you come to take this job, Mr Hislop?'

'I answered an advertisement.'

'You are sure you don't remember any particular mannerism of Mr Tonks's in connection with the radio?'

'No.'

'And you can tell me no more about your interview in the study that led to the scene in the hall?'

'No.'

'Will you please ask Mrs Tonks if she will be kind enough to speak to me for a moment?'

'Certainly,' said Hislop, and went away.

Septimus's wife came in looking like death. Alleyn got her to sit down and asked her about her movements on the preceding evening. She said she was feeling unwell and dined in her room. She went to bed immediately afterwards. She heard Septimus yelling at Phillipa and went to Phillipa's room. Septimus accused Mr Hislop and her daughter of 'terrible things'. She got as far as this and then broke down quietly. Alleyn was very gentle with her. After a little while she learned that Septimus had gone to her room with her and had continued to speak of 'terrible things'.

'What sort of things?' asked Alleyn.

'He was not responsible,' said Isabel. 'He did not know what he was saying. I think he had been drinking.'

She thought he had remained with her for perhaps a quarter of an hour. Possibly longer. He left her abruptly and she heard him go along the passage, past Phillipa's door, and presumably downstairs. She had stayed awake for a long time. The wireless could not be heard from her room. Alleyn showed her the curtain knobs, but she seemed quite unable to take in their significance. He let her go, summoned Fox, and went over the whole case.

'What's your idea on the show?' he asked when he had finished.

'Well, sir,' said Fox, in his stolid way, 'on the face of it the young gentlemen have got alibis. We'll have to check them up, of course, and I don't see we can go much further until we have done so.'

'For the moment,' said Alleyn, 'let us suppose Masters Guy and Arthur to be safely established behind cast-iron alibis. What then?'

'Then we've got the young lady, the old lady, the secretary, and the servants.'

'Let us parade them. But first let us go over the wireless game. You'll have to watch me here. I gather that the only way in which the radio could be fixed to give Mr Tonks his quietus is like this: Control knobs removed. Holes bored in front panel with fine drill. Metal knobs substituted and packed with blotting-paper to insulate them from metal shafts and make them stay put. Heavier flex from adapter to radiator cut and the ends of the wires pushed through the drilled holes to make contact with the new knobs. Thus we have a positive and negative pole. Mr Tonks bridges the gap, gets a mighty wallop as the current passes through him to the earth. The switchboard fuse is blown almost immediately. All this is rigged by murderer while Sep was upstairs bullying wife and daughter. Sep revisited study some time after ten-twenty. Whole thing was made ready between ten, when Arthur went out, and the time Sep returned – say, about ten-forty-five. The murderer reappeared, connected radiator with flex, removed wires, changed back knobs, and left the thing tuned in. Now I take it that the burst of static described by Phillipa and Hislop would be caused by the short-circuit that killed our Septimus?'

'That's right. It also affected all the heaters in the house. *Vide* Miss Tonks's radiator.'

'Yes. He put all that right again. It would be a simple enough matter for anyone who knew how. He'd just have to fix the fuse on the main switchboard. How long do you say it would take to – what's the horrible word? – to recondition the whole show?'

'M'm,' said Fox deeply. 'At a guess, sir, fifteen minutes. He'd have to be nippy.'

'Yes,' agreed Alleyn. 'He or she.'

'I don't see a female making a success of it,' grunted Fox. 'Look here, Chief, you know what I'm thinking. Why did Mr Hislop lie about deceased's habit of licking his thumbs? You say Hislop told you he remembered nothing and Chase says he overheard him saying the trick nearly drove him dippy.'

'Exactly,' said Alleyn. He was silent for so long that Fox felt moved to utter a discreet cough.

'Eh?' said Alleyn. 'Yes, Fox, yes. It'll have to be done.' He consulted the telephone directory and dialled a number.

'May I speak to Dr Meadows? Oh, it's you, is it? Do you remember Mr Hislop telling you that Septimus Tonks's trick of wetting his fingers nearly drove Hislop demented. Are you there? You don't? Sure? All right. All right. Hislop rang up at ten-twenty, you said? And you telephoned him? At eleven. Sure of the times? I see. I'd be glad if you'd come round. Can you? Well, do if you can.'

He hung up the receiver.

'Get Chase again, will you, Fox?'

Chase, recalled, was most insistent that Mr Hislop had spoken about it to Dr Meadows.

'It was when Mr Hislop had flu, sir. I went up with the doctor. Mr Hislop had a high temperature and was talking very

excited. He kept on and on, saying the master had guessed his ways had driven him crazy and that the master kept on purposely to aggravate. He said if it went on much longer he'd ...
he didn't know what he was talking about, sir, really.'

'What did he say he'd do?'

'Well, sir, he said he'd – he'd do something desperate to the master. But it was only his rambling, sir. I daresay he wouldn't remember anything about it.'

'No,' said Alleyn, 'I daresay he wouldn't.' When Chase had gone he said to Fox: 'Go and find out about those boys and their alibis. See if they can put you on to a quick means of checking up. Get Master Guy to corroborate Miss Phillipa's statement that she was locked in her room.'

Fox had been gone for some time and Alleyn was still busy with his notes when the study door burst open and in came Dr Meadows.

'Look here, my giddy sleuth-hound,' he shouted, 'what's all this about Hislop? Who says he disliked Sep's abominable habits?'

'Chase does. And don't bawl at me like that. I'm worried.'

'So am I, blast you. What are you driving at? You can't imagine that ... that poor little broken-down hack is capable of electrocuting anybody, let alone Sep?'

'I have no imagination,' said Alleyn wearily.

'I wish to God I hadn't called you in. If the wireless

killed Sep, it was because he'd monkeyed with it.'

'And put it right after it had killed him?'

Dr Meadows stared at Alleyn in silence.

'Now,' said Alleyn, 'you've got to give me a straight answer, Meadows. Did Hislop, while he was semi-delirious, say that this habit of Tonks's made him feel like murdering him?'

'I'd forgotten Chase was there,' said Dr Meadows.

'Yes, you'd forgotten that.'

'But even if he did talk wildly, Alleyn, what of it? Damn it, you can't arrest a man on the strength of a remark made in delirium.'

'I don't propose to do so. Another motive has come to light.'

'You mean – Phips – last night?'

'Did he tell you about that?'

'She whispered something to me this morning. I'm very fond of Phips. My God, are you sure of your grounds?'

'Yes,' said Alleyn. 'I'm sorry. I think you'd better go, Meadows.'

'Are you going to arrest him?'

'I have to do my job.'

There was a long silence.

'Yes,' said Dr Meadows at last. 'You have to do your job. Goodbye, Alleyn.'

Fox returned to say that Guy and Arthur had never left

their parties. He had got hold of two of their friends. Guy and Mrs Tonks confirmed the story of the locked door.

'It's a process of elimination,' said Fox. 'It must be the secretary. He fixed the radio while deceased was upstairs. He must have dodged back to whisper through the door to Miss Tonks. I suppose he waited somewhere down here until he heard deceased blow himself to blazes and then put everything straight again, leaving the radio turned on.'

Alleyn was silent.

'What do we do now, sir?' asked Fox.

'I want to see the hook inside the front door where they hang their keys.'

Fox, looking dazed, followed his superior to the little entrance hall.

'Yes, there they are,' said Alleyn. He pointed to a hook with two latch-keys hanging from it. 'You could scarcely miss them. Come on, Fox.'

Back in the study they found Hislop with Bailey in attendance.

Hislop looked from one Yard man to another.

'I want to know if it's murder.'

'We think so,' said Alleyn.

'I want you to realise that Phillipa – Miss Tonks – was locked in her room all last night.'

'Until her brother came home and unlocked the door,' said Alleyn.

'That was too late. He was dead by then.'

'How do you know when he died?'

'It must have been when there was that crash of static.'

'Mr Hislop,' said Alleyn, 'why would you not tell me how much that trick of licking his fingers exasperated you?'

'But – how do you know? I never told anyone.'

'You told Dr Meadows when you were ill.'

'I don't remember.' He stopped short. His lips trembled. Then, suddenly he began to speak.

'Very well. It's true. For two years he's tortured me. You see, he knew something about me. Two years ago when my wife was dying, I took money from the cash-box in that desk. I paid it back and thought he hadn't noticed. He knew all the time. From then on he had me where he wanted me. He used to sit there like a spider. I'd hand him a paper. He'd wet his thumbs with a clicking noise and a sort of complacent grimace. Click, click. Then he'd thumb the papers. He knew it drove me crazy. He'd look at me and then … click, click. And then he'd say something about the cash. He'd never quite accused me, just hinted. And I was impotent. You think I'm insane. I'm not. I could have murdered him. Often and often I've thought how I'd do it. Now you think I've done it. I haven't. There's the joke of it. I hadn't the pluck. And last night when Phillipa showed me she cared, it was like Heaven – unbelievable. For the first time since I've been here I *didn't* feel like killing him. And last night someone else *did*!'

He stood there trembling and vehement. Fox and Bailey, who had watched him with bewildered concern, turned to Alleyn. He was about to speak when Chase came in. 'A note for you, sir,' he said to Alleyn. 'It came by hand.'

Alleyn opened it and glanced at the first few words. He looked up.

'You may go, Mr Hislop. Now I've got what I expected – what I fished for.'

When Hislop had gone they read the letter.

Dear Alleyn,
Don't arrest Hislop. I did it. Let him go at once if you've arrested him and don't tell Phips you ever suspected him. I was in love with Isabel before she met Sep. I've tried to get her to divorce him, but she wouldn't because of the kids. Damned nonsense, but there's no time to discuss it now. I've got to be quick. He suspected us. He reduced her to a nervous wreck. I was afraid she'd go under altogether. I thought it all out. Some weeks ago I took Phips's key from the hook inside the front door. I had the tools and the flex and wire all ready. I knew where the main switchboard was and the cupboard. I meant to wait until they all went away at the New Year, but last night when Hislop rang

me I made up my mind at once. He said the boys and
servants were out and Phips locked in her room. I told
him to stay in his room and to ring me up in half an
hour if things hadn't quieted down. He didn't ring up.
I did. No answer, so I knew Sep wasn't in his study.

I came round, let myself in, and listened. All quiet
upstairs but the lamp still on in the study, so I knew he
would come down again. He'd said he wanted to get the
midnight broadcast from somewhere.

I locked myself in and got to work. When Sep
was away last year, Arthur did one of his modern
monstrosities of painting in the study. He talked about
the knobs making good pattern. I noticed then that they
were very like the ones on the radio and later on I tried
one and saw that it would fit if I packed it up a bit.
Well, I did the job just as you worked it out, and it only
took twelve minutes. Then I went into the drawing-
room and waited.

He came down from Isabel's room and evidently
went straight to the radio. I hadn't thought it would
make such a row, and half expected someone would
come down. No one came. I went back, switched off
the wireless, mended the fuse in the main switchboard,
using my torch. Then I put everything right in the study.

There was no particular hurry. No one would come
in while he was there and I got the radio going as soon

as possible to suggest he was at it. I knew I'd be called in when they found him. My idea was to tell them he had died of a stroke. I'd been warning Isabel it might happen at any time. As soon as I saw the burned hand I knew that cat wouldn't jump. I'd have tried to get away with it if Chase hadn't gone round bleating about electrocution and burned fingers. Hislop saw the hand. I daren't do anything but report the case to the police, but I thought you'd never twig the knobs. One up to you.

I might have bluffed through if you hadn't suspected Hislop. Can't let you hang the blighter. I'm enclosing a note to Isabel, who won't forgive me, and an official one for you to use. You'll find me in my bedroom upstairs. I'm using cyanide. It's quick.

I'm sorry, Alleyn. I think you knew, didn't you? I've bungled the whole game, but if you will be a super sleuth ... Goodbye.

Henry Meadows

Persons or Things Unknown

Carter Dickson

'After all,' said our host, 'it's Christmas. Why not let the skeleton out of the bag?'

'Or the cat out of the closet,' said the historian, who likes to be precise even about *clichés*. 'Are you serious?'

'Yes,' said our host 'I want to know whether it's safe for anyone to sleep in that little room at the head of the stairs.'

He had just bought the place. This party was in the nature of a house-warming; and I had already decided privately that the place needed one. It was a long, damp, high-windowed house, hidden behind a hill in Sussex. The drawing-room, where a group of us had gathered round the fire after dinner, was much too long and much too draughty. It had fine panelling – a rich brown where the firelight was always finding new gleams – and a hundred little reflections trembled down its length, as in so many small gloomy mirrors. But it remained draughty.

Of course, we all liked the house. It had the most modern of lighting and heating arrangements, though the plumbing sent ghostly noises and clanks far down into its interior whenever you turned on a tap. But the smell of the past was in it; and you could not get over the idea that somebody was following you about. Now, at the host's flat mention of a certain possibility, we all looked at our wives.

'But you never told us,' said the historian's wife, rather shocked, 'you never told us you had a ghost here!'

'I don't know that I have,' replied our host quite seriously. 'All I have is a bundle of evidence about something queer that once happened. It's all right; I haven't put anyone in that little room at the head of the stairs. So we can drop the discussion, if you'd rather.'

'You know we can't,' said the inspector: who, as a matter of strict fact, is an Assistant Commissioner of the Metropolitan Police. He smoked a large cigar, and contemplated ghosts with satisfaction. 'This is exactly the time and place to hear about it. What is it?'

'It's rather in your line,' our host told him slowly. Then

he looked at the historian. 'And in your line, too. It's a historical story. I suppose you'd call it a historical romance.'

'I probably should. What is the date?'

'The date is the year sixteen hundred and sixty.'

'That's Charles the Second, isn't it, Will?' demanded the historian's wife; she annoys him sometimes by asking these questions. 'I'm terribly fond of them. I hope it has lots of big names in it. You know: Charles the Second and Buckingham and the rest of them. I remember, when I was a little girl, going to see' – she mentioned a great actor – 'play David Garrick. I was looking forward to it. I expected to see the programme and the cast of characters positively bristling with people like Dr Johnson and Goldsmith and Burke and Gibbon and Reynolds, going in and out every minute. There wasn't a single one of them in it, and I felt swindled before the play had begun.'

The trouble was that she spoke without conviction. The historian looked sceptically over his pince-nez.

'I warn you,' he said, 'if this is something you claim to have found in a drawer, in a crabbed old handwriting and all the rest of it, I'm going to be all over you professionally. Let me hear one anachronism – '

But he spoke without conviction, too. Our host was so serious that there was a slight, uneasy silence, in the group.

'No. I didn't find it in a drawer; the parson gave it to

me. And the handwriting isn't particularly crabbed. I can't show it to you, because it's being typed, but it's a diary: a great, hefty mass of stuff. Most of it is rather dull, though I'm steeped in the seventeenth century, and I confess I enjoy it. The diary was begun in the summer of '60 – just after the Restoration – and goes on to the end of '64. It was kept by Mr Everard Poynter, who owned Manfred Manor (that's six or seven miles from here) when it was a farm.

'I know that fellow,' he added, looking thoughtfully at the fire. 'I know about him and his sciatica and his views on mutton and politics. I know why he went up to London to dance on Oliver Cromwell's grave, and I can guess who stole the two sacks of malt out of his brew-house while he was away. I see him as half a Hat; the old boy had a beaver hat he wore on his wedding day, and I'll bet he wore it to his death. It's out of all this that I got the details about people. The actual facts I got from the report of the coroner's inquest, which the parson lent me.'

'Hold on!' said the Inspector, sitting up straight. 'Did this fellow Poynter see the ghost and die?'

'No, no. Nothing like that. But he was one of the witnesses. He saw a man hacked to death, with thirteen stab wounds in his body, from a hand that wasn't there and a weapon that didn't exist.'

There was a silence.

'A murder?' asked the Inspector.

'A murder.'

'Where?'

'In that little room at the head of the stairs. It used to be called the Ladies' Withdrawing Room.'

Now, it is all very well to sit in your well-lighted flat in town and say we were hypnotised by an atmosphere. You can hear motorcars crashing their gears, or curse somebody's wireless. You did not sit in that house, with a great wind rushing up off the downs, and a wall of darkness built up for three miles around you: knowing that at a certain hour you would have to retire to your room and put out the light, completing the wall.

'I regret to say,' went on our host, 'that there are no great names. These people were no more concerned with the Court of Charles the Second – with one exception – than we are concerned with the Court of George the Sixth. They lived in a little, busy, possibly ignorant world. They were fierce, fire-eating Royalists, most of them, who cut the Stuart arms over their chimney-pieces again and only made a gala trip to town to see the regicides executed in October of '60. Poynter's diary is crowded with them. Among others there is Squire Radlow, who owned this house then and was a great friend of Poynter. There was Squire Radlow's wife, Martha, and his daughter Mary.

'Mistress Mary Radlow was seventeen years old. She

was not one of your fainting girls. Poynter – used to giving details – records that she was five feet tall, and thirty-two inches round the bust. "Pretty and delicate," Poynter says, with hazel eyes and a small mouth. But she could spin flax against any woman in the county; she once drained a pint of wine at a draught, for a wager; and she took eager pleasure in any good spectacle, like a bear-baiting or a hanging. I don't say that flippantly, but as a plain matter of fact. She was also fond of fine clothes, and danced well.

'In the summer of '60, Mistress Mary was engaged to be married to Richard Oakley, of Rawndene. Nobody seems to have known much about Oakley. There are any number of references to him in the diary, but Poynter gives up trying to make him out. Oakley was older than the girl; of genial disposition, though he wore his hair like a Puritan; and a great reader of books. He had a good estate at Rawndene, which he managed well, but his candle burned late over his books; and he wandered abroad in all weathers, summer or frost, in as black a study as the Black Man.

'You might have thought that Mistress Mary would have preferred somebody livelier. But Oakley was good enough company, by all accounts, and he suited her exactly – they tell me that wives understand this.

'And here is where the trouble enters. At the Restoration, Oakley was looking a little white. Not that his loyalty was exactly suspect; but he had bought his estate under the

Commonwealth. If sales made under the Commonwealth were now declared null and void by the new Government, it meant ruin for Oakley; and also, under the business-like standards of the time, it meant the end of his prospective marriage to Mistress Mary.

'Then Gerald Vanning appeared.

'Hoy, what a blaze he must have made! He was fresh and oiled from Versailles, from Cologne, from Bruges, from Brussels, from Breda, from everywhere he had gone in the train of the formerly exiled king. Vanning was one of those "confident young men" about whom we hear so much complaint from old-style Cavaliers in the early years of the Restoration. His family had been very powerful in Kent before the Civil Wars. Everybody knew he would be well rewarded, as he was.

'If this were a romance, I could now tell you how Mistress Mary fell in love with the handsome young Cavalier, and forgot about Oakley. But the truth seems to be that she never liked Vanning. Vanning disgusted Poynter by a habit of bowing and curvetting, with a superior smile, every time he made a remark. It is probable that Mistress Mary understood him no better than Poynter did.

'There is a description in the diary of a dinner Squire Radlow gave to welcome him here at this house. Vanning came over in a coach, despite the appalling state of the roads, with a dozen lackeys in attendance. This helped to impress the Squire, though nothing had as yet been settled on him by the new regime. Vanning already wore his hair long, whereas the others were just growing theirs. They must have looked odd and patchy, like men beginning to grow beards, and rustic enough to amuse him.

'But Mistress Mary was there. Vanning took one look at her, clapped his hand on the back of a chair, bowed, rolled up his eyes, and began to lay siege to her in the full-dress style of the French king taking a town. He slid *bons mots* on his tongue like sweetmeats; he hiccoughed; he strutted; he directed killing ogles. Squire Radlow and his wife were enraptured. They liked Oakley of Rawndene – but it was possible that Oakley might be penniless in a month. Whereas Vanning was to be heaped with prefer-ments, a matter of which he made no secret. Throughout this dinner Richard Oakley looked unhappy, and "shifted his eyes".

'When the men got drunk after dinner, Vanning spoke frankly to Squire Radlow. Oakley staggered out to get some air under the apple trees; what between liquor and crowding misfortunes, he did not feel well. Together among the fumes, Vanning and Squire Radlow shouted friendship at each other, and wept. Vanning swore he would never wed anybody but Mistress Mary, not if his soul rotted deep in hell as Oliver's. The Squire was stern, but not too stern. "Sir," said the Squire, "you abuse my hospitality; my daughter is pledged to the gentleman who has just left us; but it may be that we must speak of this presently." Poynter, though he saw the justice of the argument, went home disturbed.

'Now, Gerald Vanning was not a fool. I have seen his portrait, painted a few years later when periwigs came into fashion. It is a shiny, shrewd, razorish kind of face. He had some genuine Classical learning, and a smattering of scientific monkey tricks, the new toy of the time. But, above all, he had foresight. In the first place, he was genuinely smitten with hazel eyes and other charms. In the second place, Mistress Mary Radlow was a catch. When awarding bounty to the faithful, doubtless the King and Sir Edward Hyde would not forget Vanning of Mallingford; on the other hand, it was just possible they might.

'During the next three weeks it was almost taken for granted that Vanning should eventually become the Squire's son-in-law. Nothing was said or done, of course. But Vanning dined a dozen times here, drank with the Squire, and gave to the Squire's wife a brooch once owned by Charles the First. Mistress Mary spoke of it furiously to Poynter.

'Then the unexpected news came.

'Oakley was safe in his house and lands. An Act had been passed to confirm all sales and leases of property since the Civil Wars. It meant that Oakley was once more the well-to-do son-in-law; and the Squire could no longer object to his bargain.

'I have here an account of how this news was received at the manor. I did not get it from Poynter's diary. I got it from the records of the coroner's inquest. What astonishes us when we read these chronicles is the blunt directness, the violence, like a wind, or a pistol clapped to the head, with which people set about getting what they wanted. For, just two months afterwards, there was murder done.'

* * *

Our host paused. The room was full of the reflections of firelight. He glanced at the ceiling; what we heard up there was merely the sound of a servant walking overhead.

'Vanning,' he went on, 'seems to have taken the fact quietly enough. He was here at the manor when Oakley arrived with the news. It was five or six o'clock in the afternoon. Mistress Mary, the Squire, the Squire's wife, and Vanning were sitting in the Ladies' Withdrawing Room. This was (and is) the room at the head of the stairs – a little square place, with two 'panel' windows that would not open. It was furnished with chairs of oak and brocade; a needlework-frame; and a sideboard chastely bearing a plate of oranges, a glass jug of water, and some glasses.

'There was only one candle burning, at some distance from Vanning, so that nobody had a good view of his face. He sat in his riding-coat, with his sword across his lap. When Oakley came in with the news, he was observed to put his hand on his sword; but afterwards he "made a leg" and left without more words.

'The wedding had originally been set for the end of November; both Oakley and Mistress Mary still claimed this date. It was accepted with all the more cheerfulness by the Squire, since, in the intervening months, Vanning had not yet received any dazzling benefits. True, he had been awarded £500 a year by the Healing and Blessed Parliament. But he was little better off than Oakley; a bargain was a bargain, said the Squire, and Oakley was his own dear son. Nobody seems to know what Vanning did in the interim, except that he settled down quietly at Mallingford.

'But from this time curious rumours began to go about the countryside. They all centred round Richard Oakley. Poynter records some of them, at first evidently not even realizing their direction. They were as light as dandelion-clocks blown off, but they floated and settled.

'Who was Oakley? What did anybody know about him, except that he had come here and bought land under Oliver? He had vast learning, and above a hundred books in his house; what need did he have of that? What had he been? A parson? A doctor of letters of physic? Or letters of a more unnatural kind? Why did he go for long walks in the woods, particularly after dusk?

'Oakley, if questioned, said that this was his nature. But an honest man, meaning an ordinary man, could understand no such nature. A wood was thick; you could not tell what might be in it after nightfall; an honest man preferred the tavern. Such whispers were all the more rapid-moving because of the troubled times. The broken bones of a Revolution are not easily healed. Then there was the unnatural state of the weather. In winter there was no cold at all: the roads dusty; a swarm of flies; and the rose-bushes full of leaves into the following January.

'Oakley heard none of the rumours, or pretended to hear none. It was Jamy Achen, a lad of weak mind and therefore afraid of nothing, who saw something following Richard Oakley through Gallows Copse. The boy said he had not got a good look at it, since the time was after dusk. But he heard it rustle behind the trees, peering out at intervals after Mr Oakley. He said that it seemed human, but that he was not sure it was alive.

'On the night of Friday, the 26th November, Gerald Vanning rode over to this house alone. It was seven o'clock, a late hour for the country. He was admitted to the lower hall by Kitts, the Squire's steward, and he asked for Mr Oakley. Kitts told him that Mr Oakley was above-stairs with Mistress Mary, and that the Squire was asleep over supper with Mr Poynter.

'It is certain that Vanning was wearing no sword. Kitts held the candle high and looked at him narrowly, for he seemed on a wire of apprehension and kept glancing over his shoulder as he pulled off his gloves. He wore jack-boots, a riding-coat half-buttoned, a lace band at the neck, and a flat-crowned beaver hat with a gold band. Under his sharp nose there was a little edge of moustache, and he was sweating.

'"Mr Oakley has brought a friend with him, I think," says Vanning.

'"No, sir," says Kitts, "he is alone."

'"But I am sure his friend has followed him," says Vanning, again twitching his head round and looking over his shoulder. He also jumped as though something had touched him, and kept turning round and round and looking sharply into corners as though he were playing hide-and-seek.

'"Well!" says Mr Vanning, with a whistle of breath through his nose. "Take me to Mistress Mary. Stop! First fetch two or three brisk lads from the kitchen, and you shall go with me."

'The steward was alarmed, and asked what was the matter. Vanning would not tell him, but instructed him to see that the servants carried cudgels and lights. Four of them went above-stairs. Vanning knocked at the door of the Withdrawing Room, and was bidden to enter. The servants remained outside, and both the lights and the cudgels trembled in their hands: later they did not know why.

'As the door opened and closed, Kitts caught a glimpse of Mistress Mary sitting by the table in the rose-brocade dress she reserved usually for Sundays, and Oakley sitting on the edge of the table beside her. Both looked round as though surprised.

'Presently Kitts heard voices talking, but so low he could not make out what was said. The voices spoke more rapidly; then there was a sound of moving about. The next thing to which Kitts could testify was a noise as though a candlestick had been knocked over. There was a thud; a high-pitched kind of noise; muffled breathing sounds and a sort of thrashing on the floor; and Mistress Mary suddenly beginning to scream over it.

'Kitts and his three followers laid hold of the door, but someone had bolted it. They attacked the door in a way that roused the Squire in the dining-room below, but it held. Inside, after a silence, someone was heard to stumble and grope towards the door. Squire Radlow and Mr Poynter came running up the stairs just as the door was unbolted from inside.

'Mistress Mary was standing there, panting, with her eyes wide and staring. She was holding up one edge of her full skirt, where it was stained with blood as though someone had scoured and polished a weapon there. She cried to them to bring lights; and one of the servants held up a lantern in the doorway.

'Vanning was half-lying, half-crouching over against the far wall, with a face like oiled paper as he lifted round his head to look at them. But they were looking at Oakley, or what was left of Oakley. He had fallen near the table, with the candle smashed beside him. They could not tell how many wounds there were in Oakley's neck and body; above a dozen, Poynter thought, and he was right. Vanning stumbled over and tried to lift him up, but of course, it was too late. Now listen to Poynter's own words:

'"Mr Radlow ran to Mr Vanning and laid hold of him, crying: 'You are a murderer! You have murdered him!' Mr Vanning cried to him: 'By God and His mercy, I have not touched him! I have no sword or dagger by me!' And indeed, this was true. For he was flung down on the floor by this bloody work, and ordered to be searched, but not so much as a pin was there in his clothes.

'"I had observed by the nature of the wide, gaping wounds that some such blade as a broad knife had inflicted them, or the like. But what had done this was a puzzle, for every inch of the room did we search, high, low and turn-over; and still not so much as a pin in crack or crevice.

'"Mr Vanning deposed that as he was speaking with Mr

Oakley, something struck out the light, and overthrew Mr Oakley, and knelt on his chest. But who or what this was, or where it had gone when the light was brought, he could not say.'"

* * *

Bending close to the firelight, our host finished reading the notes from the sheet of paper in his hands. He folded up the paper, put it back in his pocket, and looked at us.

The historian's wife, who had drawn closer to her husband, shifted uneasily. 'I wish you wouldn't tell us these things,' she complained. 'But tell us, anyway. I still don't understand. What was the man killed with, then?'

'That,' said our host, lighting his pipe, 'is the question. If you accept natural laws as governing this world, there wasn't anything that could have killed him. Look here a moment!'

(For we were all looking at the ceiling.)

'The Squire begged Mistress Mary to tell him what had happened. First she began to whimper a little, and for the first time in her life she fainted. The Squire wanted to throw some water over her, but Vanning carried her downstairs and they forced brandy between her teeth. When she recovered she was a trifle wandering, with no story at all.

'Something had put out the light. There had been a sound like a fall and a scuffling. Then the noise of moving about, and the smell of blood in a close, confined room. Something seemed to be plucking or pulling at her skirts. She does not appear to have remembered anything more.

'Of course, Vanning was put under restraint, and a magistrate sent for. They gathered in this room, which was a good deal bleaker and barer than it is today; but they pinned Vanning in the chimney corner of that fire-place. The Squire drew his sword and attempted to run Vanning through: while both of them wept, as the fashion was. But Poynter ordered two of the lads to hold the Squire back, quoting himself later as saying: "This must be done in good order."

'Now, what I want to impress on you is that these people were not fools. They had possibly a cruder turn of thought and speech; but they were used to dealing with realities like wood and beef and leather. Here was a reality. Oakley's wounds were six inches deep and an inch wide, from a thick, flat blade that in places had scraped the bone. But there wasn't any such blade, and they knew it.

'Four men stood in the door and held lights while they searched for that knife (if there was such a thing): and they didn't find it. They pulled the room to pieces; and they didn't find it. Nobody could have whisked it out, past the men in the door. The windows didn't open, being set into the wall like panels, so nobody could have got rid of the knife there. There was only one door, outside which the servants had been standing. Something had cut a man to pieces; yet it simply wasn't there.

'Vanning, pale but calmer, repeated his account. Questioned as to why he had come to the house that night, he answered that there had been a matter to settle with Oakley. Asked what it was, he said he had not liked the conditions in his own home for the past month: he would beg Mr Oakley to mend them. He had done Mr Oakley no harm, beyond trying to take a bride from him, and therefore he would ask Mr Oakley to call off his dogs. What dogs? Vanning explained that he did not precisely mean dogs. He meant something that had got into his bedroom cupboard, but was only there at night; and he had reasons for thinking Mr Oakley had whistled it there. It had been there only since he had been paying attentions to Mistress Mary.

'These men were only human. Poynter ordered the steward to go up and search the little room again – and the steward wouldn't go.

'That little seed of terror had begun to grow like a mango-tree under a cloth, and push up the cloth and stir out tentacles. It was easy to forget the broad, smiling face of Richard Oakley, and to remember the curious "shifting" of his eyes. When you recalled that, after all, Oakley was twice Mistress Mary's age, you might begin to wonder just whom you had been entertaining at bread and meat.

'Even Squire Radlow did not care to go upstairs again in his own house. Vanning, sweating and squirming in the chimney corner, plucked up courage as a confident young man and volunteered to go. They let him. But no sooner had he got into the little room than the door clapped again, and he came out running. It was touch-and-go whether they would desert the house in a body.'

Again our host paused. In the silence it was the Inspector who spoke, examining his cigar and speaking with some scepticism. He had a commonsense voice, which restored reasonable values.

'Look here,' he said, 'are you telling us local bogy-tales, or are you seriously putting this forward as evidence?'

'As evidence given at a coroner's inquest.'

'Reliable evidence?'

'I believe so.'

'I don't,' returned the Inspector, drawing the air through a hollow tooth. 'After all, I suppose we've got to admit that a man was murdered, since there was an inquest. But if he died of being hacked or slashed with thirteen wounds, some instrument made those wounds. What happened to that weapon? You say it wasn't in the room; but how do we know that? How do we know it wasn't hidden away somewhere, and they simply couldn't find it?'

'I think I can give you my word,' said our host slowly, 'that no weapon was hidden there.'

'Then what the devil happened to it? A knife at least six inches in the blade, and an inch broad – '

'Yes. But the fact is, nobody could see it.'

'It wasn't hidden anywhere, and yet nobody could see it?'

'That's right.'

'An invisible weapon?'

'Yes,' answered our host, with a curious shining in his eyes. 'A quite literally invisible weapon.'

'How do you know?' demanded his wife abruptly.

Hitherto she had taken no part in the conversation. But she had been studying him in an odd way, sitting on a hassock; and, as he hesitated, she rose at him in a glory of accusation.

'You villain!' she cried. 'Ooh, you unutterable villain! You've been making it all up! Just to make everybody afraid to go to bed, and because *I* didn't know anything about the place, you've been telling us a pack of lies – '

But he stopped her.

'No. If I had been making it up, I should have told you it was a story.' Again he hesitated, almost biting his nails. 'I'll admit that I may have been trying to mystify you a bit. That's reasonable, because I honestly don't know the truth myself. I can make a guess at it, that's all. I can make a guess at how those wounds came there. But that isn't the real problem. That isn't what bothers me, don't you see?'

Here the historian intervened. 'A wide acquaintance with sensational fiction,' he said, 'gives me the line on which you're working. I submit that the victim was stabbed with an icicle, as in several tales I could mention. Afterwards the ice melted – and was, in consequence, an invisible weapon.'

'No,' said our host.

'I mean,' he went on, 'that it's not feasible. You would hardly find an icicle in such unnaturally warm weather as they were having. And icicles are brittle: you wouldn't get a flat, broad icicle of such steel-strength and sharpness that thirteen stabs could be made and the bone scraped in some of them. And an icicle isn't invisible. Under the circumstances, this knife was invisible – despite its size.'

'Bosh!' said the historian's wife. 'There isn't any such thing.'

'There is if you come to think about it. Of course, it's only an idea of mine, and it may be all wrong. Also, as I say, it's not the real problem, though it's so closely associated with the real problem that –

'But you haven't heard the rest of the story. Shall I conclude it?'

'By all means.'

'I am afraid there are no great alarms or sensations,' our

host went on, 'though the very name of Richard Oakley became a nightmare to keep people indoors at night. "Oakley's friend" became a local synonym for anything that might get you if you didn't look sharp. One or two people saw him walking in the woods afterwards, his head was on one side and the stab wounds were still there.

'A grand jury of Sussex gentlemen, headed by Sir Benedict Skene, completely exonerated Gerald Vanning. The coroner's jury had already said "persons or things unknown", and added words of sympathy with Mistress Mary to the effect that she was luckily quit of a dangerous bargain. It may not surprise you to hear that eighteen months after Oakley's death she married Vanning.

'She was completely docile, though her old vivacity had gone. In those days young ladies did not remain spinsters through choice. She smiled, nodded, and made the proper responses, though it seems probable that she never got over what had happened.

'Matters became settled, even humdrum. Vanning waxed prosperous and respectable. His subsequent career I have had to look up in other sources, since Poynter's diary breaks off at the end of '64. But a grateful Government made him Sir Gerald Vanning, Bart. He became a leading member of the Royal Society, tinkering with the toys of science. His cheeks filled out, the slyness left his eyes, a periwig adorned his head, and four Flanders mares

drew his coach to Gresham House. At home he often chose
this house to live in when Squire Radlow died; he moved
between here and Mallingford with the soberest grace.
The little room, once such a cause of terror, he seldom
visited; but its door was not locked.

'His wife saw to it that these flagstones were kept
scrubbed, and every stick of wood shining. She was a
good wife. He for his part was a good husband: he treated
her well and drank only for his thirst, though she often
pressed him to drink more than he did. It is at this pitch
of domesticity that we get the record of another coroner's
inquest.

'Vanning's throat was cut on the night of the 5th
October, '67.

'On an evening of high winds, he and his wife came
here from Mallingford. He was in unusually good spirits,
having just done a profitable piece of business. They had
supper together, and Vanning drank a great deal. His wife
kept him company at it. (Didn't I tell you she once drank
off a pint of wine at a draught, for a wager?) She said it
would make him sleep soundly; for it seems to be true that
he sometimes talked in his sleep. At eight o'clock, she tells
us, she went up to bed, leaving him still at the table. At
what time he went upstairs we do not know, and neither
do the servants. Kitts, the steward, thought he heard him
stumbling up that staircase out there at a very late hour.

Kitts also thought he heard someone crying out, but a high October gale was blowing and he could not be sure.

'On the morning of the 6th October, a cowherd named Coates was coming round the side of this house in a sodden daybreak from which the storm had just cleared. He was on his way to the west meadow, and stopped to drink at a rain-water barrel under the eaves just below the little room at the head of the stairs. As he was about to drink, he noticed a curious colour in the water. Looking up to find out how it had come there, he saw Sir Gerald Vanning's face looking down at him under the shadow of the yellow trees. Sir Gerald's head was sticking out of the window, and did not move; neither did the eyes. Some of the glass in the window was still intact, though his head had been run through it, and – '

It was at this point that the Inspector uttered an exclamation.

It was an exclamation of enlightenment. Our host looked at him with a certain grimness, and nodded.

'Yes,' he said. 'You know the truth now, don't you?'

'The truth?' repeated the historian's wife, almost screaming with perplexity. 'The truth about what?'

'About the murder of Oakley,' said our host. 'About the trick Vanning used to murder Oakley seven years before.

'I'm fairly sure he did it,' our host went on, nodding reflectively. 'Nothing delighted the people of that time so much as tricks and gadgets of that very sort. A clock that ran by rolling bullets down an inclined plane; a diving bell; a burglar-alarm; the Royal Society played with all of them. And Vanning (study his portrait one day) profited by the monkey-tricks he learned in exile. He invented an invisible knife.'

'But see here – !' protested the historian.

'Of course he planned the whole thing against Oakley. Oakley was no more a necromancer or a consorter with devils than I am. All those rumours about him were started with a definite purpose by Vanning himself. A crop of whispers, a weak-minded lad to be bribed, the whole power of suggestion set going; and Vanning was ready for business.

'On the given night he rode over to this house, alone, with a certain kind of knife in his pocket. He made a great show of pretending he was chased by imaginary monsters, and he alarmed the steward. With the servants for witnesses, he went upstairs to see Oakley and Mistress Mary. He bolted the door. He spoke pleasantly to them. When he had managed to distract the girl's attention, he knocked out the light, tripped up Oakley, and set upon him with that certain kind of knife. There had to be many wounds and much blood, so he could later account for blood on himself. The girl was too terrified in the dark to move. He had only to clean his knife on a soft but stiff-brocaded gown, and then put down the knife in full view. Nobody noticed it.'

The historian blinked. 'Admirable!' he said. 'Nobody noticed it, eh? Can you tell me the sort of blade that can be placed in full view without anybody noticing it?'

'Yes,' said our host. 'A blade made of ordinary plain glass, placed in the large glass jug full of water standing on a sideboard table.'

There was a silence.

'I told you about that glass water jug. It was a familiar fixture. Nobody examines a transparent jug of water.

'Vanning could have made a glass knife with the crudest of cutting tools; and glass is murderous stuff – strong, flat, sharp-edged, and as sharp-pointed as you want to make it. There was only candle-light, remember. Any minute traces of blood that might be left on the glass knife would sink as sediment in the water, while everybody looked straight at the weapon in the water and never noticed it. But Vanning (you also remember?) prevented Squire Radlow from throwing water on the girl when she fainted. Instead he carried her downstairs. Afterwards he told an admirable series of horror-tales; he found an excuse to go back to the room again alone, slip the knife into his sleeve, and get rid of it in the confusion.'

The Inspector frowned thoughtfully. 'But the real problem – ' he said.

'Yes. If that was the way it was done, did the wife know? Vanning talked in his sleep, remember.'

We looked at each other. The historian's wife, after a glance round, asked the question that was in our minds.

'And what was the verdict of *that* inquest?'

'Oh, that was simple,' said our host. 'Death by misadventure, from falling through a window while drunk and cutting his throat on the glass. Somebody observed that there were marks of heels on the board floor as though he might have been dragged there; but this wasn't insisted on. Mistress Mary lived on in complete happiness, and died at the ripe age of eighty-six, full of benevolence and sleep. These are natural explanations. Everything is natural. There's nothing wrong with that little room at the head of the stairs. It's been turned into a bedroom now; I assure you it's comfortable; and anyone who cares to sleep there is free to do so. But at the same time – '

'Quite,' we said.

The Case Is Altered

Margery Allingham

Mr Albert Campion, sitting in a first-class smoking compartment, was just reflecting sadly that an atmosphere of stultifying decency could make even Christmas something of a stuffed-owl occasion, when a new hogskin suitcase of distinctive design hit him on the knees. At that same moment a golf bag bruised the shins of the shy young man opposite, an armful of assorted magazines burst over the pretty girl in the far corner, and a blast of icy air swept round the carriage. There was the familiar rattle and lurch which indicates that the train has started at last, a squawk from a receding porter, and Lance Feering arrived before him apparently by rocket.

'Caught it,' said the newcomer with the air of one confidently expecting congratulations, but as the train bumped jerkily he teetered back on his heels and collapsed between the two young people on the opposite seat.

'My dear chap, so we noticed,' murmured Campion, and he smiled apologetically at the girl, now disentangling herself from the shellburst of newsprint. It was his own disarming my-poor-friend-is-afflicted variety of smile that he privately considered infallible, but on this occasion it let him down.

The girl, who was in the early twenties and was slim and fair, with eyes like licked brandy-balls, as Lance Feering inelegantly put it afterwards, regarded him with grave interest. She stacked the magazines into a neat bundle and placed them on the seat opposite before returning to her own book. Even Mr Feering, who was in one of his more exuberant moods, was aware of that chilly protest. He began to apologise.

Campion had known Feering in his student days, long before he had become one of the foremost designers of stage decors in Europe, and was used to him, but now even he was impressed. Lance's apologies were easy but also abject. He collected his bag, stowed it on a clear space on the rack above the shy young man's head, thrust his golf things under the seat, positively blushed when he claimed his magazines, and regarded the girl with pathetic humility. She glanced at him when he spoke, nodded coolly with just enough graciousness not to be gauche, and turned over a page.

Campion was secretly amused. At the top of his form Lance was reputed to be irresistible. His dark face with the long mournful nose and bright eyes were unhandsome enough to be interesting and the quick gestures of his short painter's hands made his conversation picturesque. His singular lack of success on this occasion clearly astonished him and he sat back in his corner eyeing the young woman with covert mistrust.

Campion resettled himself to the two hours' rigid silence which etiquette demands from first-class travellers who, although they are more than probably going to be asked to dance a reel together if not to share a bathroom only a few hours hence, have not yet been introduced.

There was no way of telling if the shy young man and the girl with the brandy-ball eyes knew each other, and whether they too were en route for Underhill, Sir Philip Cookham's Norfolk place. Campion was inclined to regard the coming festivities with a certain amount of lugubrious curiosity. Cookham himself was a magnificent old boy, of course, 'one of the more valuable pieces in the Cabinet', as someone had once said of him, but Florence was a different kettle of fish. Born to wealth and breeding, she had grown blasé towards both of them and now took her delight in notabilities, a dangerous affectation in Campion's experience. She was some sort of remote aunt of his.

He glanced again at the young people, caught the boy unaware, and was immediately interested.

The illustrated magazine had dropped from the young man's hand and he was looking out of the window, his mouth drawn down at the corners and a narrow frown between his thick eyebrows. It was not an unattractive face, too young for strong character but decent and open enough in the ordinary way. At that particular moment, however, it wore a revealing expression. There was recklessness in the twist of the mouth and sullenness in the eyes, while the hand which lay upon the inside arm-rest was clenched.

Campion was curious. Young people do not usually go away for Christmas in this top-step-at-the-dentist's frame of mind. The girl looked up from her book.

'How far is Underhill from the station?' she inquired.

'Five miles. They'll meet us.' The shy young man turned to her so easily and with such obvious affection that any romantic theory Campion might have formed was knocked on the head instantly. The youngster's troubles evidently had nothing to do with love.

Lance had raised his head with bright-eyed interest at the gratuitous information and now a faintly sardonic expression appeared upon his lips. Campion sighed for him. For a man who fell in and out of love with the abandonment of a seal round a pool, Lance Feering was an impossible optimist. Already he was regarding the girl with that shy despair which so many ladies had found too piteous to be allowed to persist. Campion washed his hands of him and turned away just in time to notice a stranger glancing in at them from the corridor. It was a dark and arrogant young face and he recognized it instantly, feeling at the same time a deep wave of sympathy for old Cookham. Florence, he gathered, had done it again.

Young Victor Preen, son of old Preen of the Preen Aero Company, was certainly notable, not to say notorious. He had obtained much publicity in his short life for his sensational flights, but a great deal more for adventures less creditable; and when angry old gentlemen in the armchairs of exclusive clubs let themselves go about the blackguardliness of the younger generation, it was very often of Victor Preen that they were thinking.

He stood now a little to the left of the compartment window, leaning idly against the wall, his chin up and his heavy lids drooping. At first sight he did not appear to be taking any interest in the occupants of the compartment, but when the shy young man looked up, Campion happened to see the swift glance of recognition, and of something else, which passed between them. Presently, still with the same elaborate casualness, the man in the corridor wandered away, leaving the other staring in front of him, the same sullen expression still in his eyes.

The incident passed so quickly that it was impossible to define the exact nature of that second glance, but Campion was never a man to go imagining things, which was why he was surprised when they arrived at Minstree station to hear Henry Boule, Florence's private secretary, introducing the two and to notice that they met as strangers.

It was pouring with rain as they came out of the station, and Boule, who, like all Florence's secretaries, appeared to be suffering from an advanced case of nerves, bundled them all into two big Daimlers, a smaller car and a shooting-brake. Campion looked round him at Florence's Christmas bag with some dismay. She had surpassed herself. Besides Lance there were at least half a dozen celebrities: a brace of political high-lights, an angry-looking lady novelist, Nadja from the ballet, a startled R.A., and Victor Preen, as well as some twelve or thirteen unfamiliar faces who looked as if they might belong to Art, Money, or even mere Relations.

Campion became separated from Lance and was looking for him anxiously when he saw him at last in one of the cars, with the novelist on one side and the girl with brandy-ball eyes on the other, Victor Preen making up the ill-assorted four.

Since Campion was an unassuming sort of person he was relegated to the brake with Boule himself, the shy young man and the whole of the luggage. Boule introduced them awkwardly and collapsed into a seat, wiping the beads from off his forehead with a relief which was a little too blatant to be tactful.

Campion, who had learned that the shy young man's name was Peter Groome, made a tentative inquiry of him as they sat jolting shoulder to shoulder in the back of the car. He nodded.

'Yes, it's the same family,' he said. 'Cookham's sister married a brother of my father's. I'm some sort of relation, I suppose.'

The prospect did not seem to fill him with any great enthusiasm and once again Campion's curiosity was piqued. Young Mr Groome was certainly not in seasonable mood.

In the ordinary way Campion would have dismissed the matter from his mind, but there was something about the youngster which attracted him, something indefinable and of a despairing quality, and moreover there had been that curious intercepted glance in the train.

They talked in a desultory fashion throughout the uncomfortable journey. Campion learned that young Groome was in his father's firm of solicitors, that he was engaged to be married to the girl with the brandy-ball eyes, who was a Miss Patricia Bullard of an old north country family, and that he thought Christmas was a waste of time.

'I hate it,' he said with a sudden passionate intensity which startled even his mild inquisitor. 'All this sentimental good-will-to-all-men-business is false and sickening. There's no such thing as good-will. The world's rotten.'

He blushed as soon as he had spoken and turned away.

'I'm sorry' he murmured, 'but all this bogus Dickensian stuff makes me writhe.'

Campion made no direct comment. Instead he asked with affable inconsequence, 'Was that young Victor Preen I saw in the other car?'

Peter Groome turned his head and regarded him with the steady stare of the wilfully obtuse.

'I was introduced to someone with a name like that, I think,' he said carefully. 'He was a little baldish man, wasn't he?'

'No, that's Sir George.' The secretary leaned over the luggage to give the information. 'Preen is the tall young man, rather handsome, with the very curling hair. He's *the* Preen, you know.' He sighed. 'It seems very young to be a millionaire, doesn't it?'

'Obscenely so,' said Mr Peter Groome abruptly, and returned to his despairing contemplation of the landscape.

Underhill was *en fête* to receive them. As soon as Campion observed the preparations, his sympathy for young Mr Groome increased, for to a jaundiced eye Lady Florence's display might well have proved as dispiriting as Preen's bank balance. Florence had 'gone all Dickens', as she said herself at the top of her voice, linking her arm through Campion's, clutching the R.A. with her free hand, and capturing Lance with a bright birdlike eye.

The great Jacobean house was festooned with holly. An eighteen-foot tree stood in the great hall. Yule logs blazed on iron dogs in the wide hearths and already the atmosphere was thick with that curious Christmas smell which is part cigar smoke and part roasting food.

Sir Philip Cookham stood receiving his guests with pathetic bewilderment. Every now and again his features broke into a smile of genuine welcome as he saw a face he knew. He was a distinguished-looking old man with a fine head and eyes permanently worried by his country's troubles.

'My dear boy, delighted to see you. Delighted,' he said, grasping Campion's hand. 'I'm afraid you've been put over in the Dower House. Did Florence tell you? She said you wouldn't mind, but I insisted that Feering went over there with you and also young Peter.' He sighed and brushed away the visitor's hasty reassurances. 'I don't know why the dear girl never feels she has a party unless the house is so overcrowded that our best friends have to sleep in the annex,' he said sadly.

The 'dear girl', looking not more than fifty-five or her

sixty years, was clinging to the arm of the lady novelist at that particular moment and the two women were emitting mirthless parrot cries at each other. Cookham smiled.

'She's happy, you know,' he said indulgently. 'She enjoys this sort of thing. Unfortunately I have a certain amount of urgent work to do this weekend, but we'll get in a chat, Campion, some time over the holiday. I want to hear your news. You're a lucky fellow. You can tell your adventures.'

The lean man grimaced. 'More secret sessions, sir?' he inquired.

The Cabinet Minister threw up his hands in a comic but expressive little gesture before he turned to greet the next guest.

As he dressed for dinner in his comfortable room in the small Georgian dower house across the park, Campion was inclined to congratulate himself on his quarters. Underhill itself was a little too much of the ancient monument for strict comfort.

He had reached the tie stage when Lance appeared. He came in very elegant indeed and highly pleased with himself. Campion diagnosed the symptoms immediately and remained irritatingly incurious.

Lance sat down before the open fire and stretched his sleek legs.

'It's not even as if I were a good-looking blighter, you know,' he observed invitingly when the silence had become irksome to him. 'In fact, Campion, when I consider myself I simply can't understand it. Did I so much as speak to the girl?'

'I don't know,' said Campion, concentrating on his dressing. 'Did you?'

'No.' Lance was passionate in his denial. 'Not a word. The hard-faced female with the inky fingers and the walrus mustache was telling me her life story all the way home in the car. This dear little poppet with the eyes was nothing more than a warm bundle at my side. I give you my dying oath on that. And yet – well, it's extraordinary, isn't it?'

Campion did not turn round. He could see the artist quite well through the mirror in front of him. Lance had a sheet of note-paper in his hand and was regarding it with that mixture of feigned amusement and secret delight which was typical of his eternally youthful spirit.

'Extraordinary,' he repeated, glancing at Campion's unresponsive back. 'She had nice eyes. Like licked brandy-balls.'

'Exactly,' agreed the lean man by the dressing table. 'I thought she seemed very taken up with her fiancé, young Master Groome, though,' he added tactlessly.

'Well, I noticed that, you know,' Lance admitted,

forgetting his professions of disinterest. 'She hardly recognized my existence in the train. Still, there's absolutely no accounting for women. I've studied 'em all my life and never understood 'em yet. I mean to say, take this case in point. That kid ignored me, avoided me, looked through me. And yet look at this. I found it in my room when I came up to change just now.'

Campion took the note with a certain amount of distaste. Lovely women were invariably stooping to folly, it seemed, but even so he could not accustom himself to the spectacle. The message was very brief. He read it at a glance and for the first time that day he was conscious of that old familiar flicker down the spine as his experienced nose smelled trouble. He re-read the five lines:

'"There is a sundial on a stone pavement just off the drive. We saw it from the car. I'll wait ten minutes there for you half an hour after the party breaks up tonight."'

There was neither signature nor initial, and the summons broke off as baldly as it had begun.

'Amazing, isn't it?' Lance had the grace to look shamefaced.

'Astounding.' Campion's tone was flat. 'Staggering, old boy. Er – fishy.'

'Fishy?'

'Yes, don't you think so?' Campion was turning over the single sheet thoughtfully and there was no amusement in the pale eyes behind his horn-rimmed spectacles. 'How did it arrive?'

'In an unaddressed envelope. I don't suppose she caught my name. After all, there must be some people who don't know it yet.' Lance was grinning impudently. 'She's batty, of course. Not safe out and all the rest of it. But I liked her eyes and she's very young.'

Campion perched himself on the edge of the table. He was still very serious.

'It's disturbing, isn't it?' he said. 'Not nice. Makes one wonder.'

'Oh, I don't know.' Lance retrieved his property and tucked it into his pocket. 'She's young and foolish, and it's Christmas.'

Campion did not appear to have heard him. 'I wonder,' he said. 'I should keep the appointment, I think. It may be unwise to interfere, but yes, I rather think I should.'

'You're telling me.' Lance was laughing. 'I may be wrong, of course,' he added defensively, 'but I think that's a cry for help. The poor girl evidently saw that I looked a dependable sort of chap and – er – having her back against the wall for some reason or other she turned instinctively to the stranger with the kind face. Isn't that how you read it?'

'Since you press me, no. Not exactly,' said Campion, and as they walked over to the house together he remained thoughtful and irritatingly uncommunicative.

Florence Cookham excelled herself that evening. Her guests were exhorted 'to be young again', with the inevitable result that Underhill contained a company of irritated and exhausted people long before midnight.

One of her ladyship's more erroneous beliefs was that she was a born organizer, and that the real secret of entertaining people lay in giving everyone something to do. Thus Lance and the R.A. – now even more startled-looking than ever – found themselves superintending the decoration of the great tree, while the girl with the brandy-ball eyes conducted a small informal dance in the drawing-room, the lady novelist scowled over the bridge table, and the ballet star refused flatly to arrange amateur theatricals.

Only two people remained exempt from this tyranny. One was Sir Philip himself, who looked in every now and again, ready to plead urgent work awaiting him in his study whenever his wife pounced upon him, and the other was Mr Campion, who had work to do on his own account and had long mastered the difficult art of self-effacement. Experience had taught him that half the secret of this manoeuvre was to keep discreetly on the move and he strolled from one party to another, always ready to look as if he belonged to any one of them should his hostess's eye ever come to rest upon him inquiringly.

For once his task was comparatively simple. Florence

was in her element as she rushed about surrounded by breathless assistants, and at one period the very air in her vicinity seemed to have become thick with coloured paper-wrappings, yards of red ribbons and a coloured snowstorm of little address tickets as she directed the packing of the presents for the Tenants' Tree, a second monster which stood in the ornamental barn beyond the kitchens.

Campion left Lance to his fate, which promised to be six or seven hours' hard labour at the most moderate estimate, and continued his purposeful meandering. His lean figure drifted among the company with an apparent aimlessness which was deceptive. There was hidden urgency in his lazy movements and his pale eyes behind his spectacles were inquiring and unhappy.

He found Patricia Bullard dancing with young Preen and paused to watch them as they swung gracefully by him. The man was in a somewhat flamboyant mood, flashing his smile and his noisy witticisms about him after the fashion of his kind, but the girl was not so content. As Campion caught sight of her pale face over her partner's sleek shoulder his eyebrows rose. For an instant he almost believed in Lance's unlikely suggestion. The girl actually did look as though she had her back to the wall. She was watching the doorway nervously and her shiny eyes were afraid.

Campion looked about him for the other young man who should have been present, but Peter Groome was not in the ballroom, nor in the great hall, nor yet among the bridge tables in the drawing-room, and half an hour later he had still not put in an appearance.

Campion was in the hall himself when he saw Patricia slip into the anteroom which led to Sir Philip's private study, that holy of holies which even Florence treated with a wholesome awe. Campion had paused for a moment to enjoy the spectacle of Lance, wild-eyed and tight-lipped, wrestling with the last of the blue glass balls and tinsel streamers on the Guests' Tree, when he caught sight of the flare of her silver skirt disappearing round a familiar doorway under one branch of the huge double staircase.

It was what he had been waiting for, and yet when it came his disappointment was unexpectedly acute, for he too had liked her smile and her brandy-ball eyes. The door was ajar when he reached it, and he pushed it open an inch or so farther, pausing on the threshold to consider the scene within. Patricia was on her knees before the panelled door which led into the inner room and was trying somewhat ineffectually to peer through the keyhole.

Campion stood looking at her regretfully, and when she straightened herself and paused to listen, with every line of her young body taut with the effort of concentration, he did not move.

Sir Philip's voice amid the noisy chatter behind him startled him, however, and he swung round to see the old man talking to a group on the other side of the room. A moment later the girl brushed past him and hurried away.

Campion went quietly into the anteroom. The study door was still closed and he moved over to the enormous period fireplace which stood beside it. This particular fireplace, with its carved and painted front, its wrought iron dogs and deeply recessed inglenooks, was one of the showpieces of Underhill.

At the moment the fire had died down and the interior of the cavern was dark, warm, and inviting. Campion stepped inside and sat down on the oak settle, where the shadows swallowed him. He had no intention of being unduly officious, but his quick ears had caught a faint sound in the inner room and Sir Philip's private sanctum was no place for furtive movements when its master was out of the way. He had not long to wait.

A few moments later the study door opened very quietly and someone came out. The newcomer moved across the room with a nervous, unsteady tread, and paused abruptly, his back to the quiet figure in the inglenook.

Campion recognized Peter Groome and his thin mouth narrowed. He was sorry. He had liked the boy.

The youngster stood irresolute. He had his hands behind him, holding in one of them a flamboyant parcel wrapped in the colored paper and scarlet ribbon which littered the house. A sound from the hall seemed to fluster him, for he spun round, thrust the parcel into the inglenook which was the first hiding place to present itself, and returned to face the new arrival. It was the girl again. She came slowly across the room, her hands outstretched and her face raised to Peter's.

In view of everything, Campion thought it best to stay where he was, nor had he time to do anything else. She was speaking urgently, passionate sincerity in her low voice.

'Peter, I've been looking for you. Darling, there's something I've got to say and if I'm making an idiotic mistake then you've got to forgive me. Look here, you wouldn't go and do anything silly, would you? Would you, Peter? Look at me.'

'My dear girl.' He was laughing unsteadily and not very convincingly with his arms around her. 'What on earth are you talking about?'

She drew back from him and peered earnestly into his face.

'You wouldn't, would you? Not even if it meant an awful lot. Not even if for some reason or other you felt you *had* to. Would you?'

He turned from her helplessly, a great weariness in the lines of his sturdy back, but she drew him round, forcing him to face her.

'Would he what, my dear?'

Florence's arch inquiry from the doorway separated them so hurriedly that she laughed delightedly and came briskly into the room, her gray curls a trifle dishevelled and her draperies flowing.

'Too divinely young. I love it!' she said devastatingly. 'I must kiss you both. Christmas is the time for love and youth and all the other dear charming things, isn't it? That's why I adore it. But, my dears, not here. Not in this silly poky little room. Come along and help me, both of you, and then you can slip away and dance together later on. But don't come in this room. This is Philip's dull part of the house. Come along this minute. Have you seen my precious tree? Too incredibly distinguished, my darlings, with two great artists at work on it. You shall both tie on a candle. Come along.'

She swept them away like an avalanche. No protest was possible. Peter shot a single horrified glance towards the fireplace, but Florence was gripping his arm; he was thrust out into the hall and the door closed firmly behind him.

Campion was left in his corner with the parcel less than a dozen feet away from him on the opposite bench. He moved over and picked it up. It was a long flat package wrapped in holly-printed tissue. Moreover, it was unexpectedly heavy and the ends were unbound.

He turned it over once or twice, wrestling with a strong

disinclination to interfere, but a vivid recollection of the girl with the brandy-ball eyes, in her silver dress, her small pale face alive with anxiety, made up his mind for him and, sighing, he pulled the ribbon.

The typewritten folder which fell on to his knees surprised him at first, for it was not at all what he had expected, nor was its title, 'Report on Messrs. Anderson and Coleridge, Messrs. Saunders, Duval and Berry, and Messrs. Birmingham and Rose,' immediately enlightening, and when he opened it at random a column of incomprehensible figures confronted him. It was a scribbled pencil note in a precise hand at the foot of one of the pages which gave him his first clue.

'These figures are estimated by us to be a reliable forecast of this firm's full working capacity.'

Two hours later it was bitterly cold in the garden and a thin white mist hung over the dark shrubbery which lined the drive when Mr Campion, picking his way cautiously along the clipped grass verge, came quietly down to the sundial walk. Behind him the gabled roofs of Underhill were shadowy against a frosty sky. There were still a few lights in the upper windows, but below stairs the entire place was in darkness.

Campion hunched his greatcoat about him and plodded on, unwonted severity in the lines of his thin face.

He came upon the sundial walk at last and paused,

straining his eyes to see through the mist. He made out the figure standing by the stone column, and heaved a sigh of relief as he recognized the jaunty shoulders of the Christmas tree decorator. Lance's incurable romanticism was going to be useful at last, he reflected with wry amusement.

He did not join his friend but withdrew into the shadows of a great clump of rhododendrons and composed himself to wait. He intensely disliked the situation in which he found himself. Apart from the extreme physical discomfort involved, he had a natural aversion towards the project on hand, but little fair-haired girls with shiny eyes can be very appealing.

It was a freezing vigil. He could hear Lance stamping about in the mist, swearing softly to himself, and even that supremely comic phenomenon had its unsatisfactory side.

They were both shivering and the mist's damp fingers seemed to have stroked their very bones when at last Campion stiffened. He had heard a rustle behind him and presently there was a movement in the wet leaves, followed by the sharp ring of feet on the stones. Lance swung round immediately, only to drop back in astonishment as a tall figure bore down.

'Where is it?'

Neither the words nor the voice came as a complete

surprise to Campion, but the unfortunate Lance was taken entirely off his guard.

'Why, hello, Preen,' he said involuntarily. 'What the devil are you doing here?'

The newcomer had stopped in his tracks, his face a white blur in the uncertain light. For a moment he stood perfectly still and then, turning on his heel, he made off without a word.

'Ah, but I'm afraid it's not quite so simple as that, my dear chap.'

Campion stepped out of his friendly shadows and as the younger man passed, slipped an arm through his and swung him round to face the startled Lance, who was coming up at the double.

'You can't clear off like this,' he went on, still in the same affable, conversational tone. 'You have something to give Peter Groome, haven't you? Something he rather wants?'

'Who the hell are you?' Preen jerked up his arm as he spoke and might have wrenched himself free had it not been for Lance, who had recognized Campion's voice and, although completely in the dark, was yet quick enough to grasp certain essentials.

'That's right, Preen,' he said, seizing the man's other arm in a bear's hug. 'Hand it over. Don't be a fool. Hand it over.'

This line of attack appeared to be inspirational, since they felt the powerful youngster stiffen between them.

'Look here, how many people know about this?'

'The world – ' Lance was beginning cheerfully when Campion forestalled him.

'We three and Peter Groome,' he said quietly. 'At the moment Sir Philip has no idea that Messrs. Preen's curiosity concerning the probable placing of Government orders for aircraft parts has overstepped the bounds of common sense. You're acting alone, I suppose?'

'Oh, lord, yes, of course.' Preen was cracking dangerously, 'If my old man gets to hear of this I – oh, well, I might as well go and crash.'

'I thought so.' Campion sounded content. 'Your father has a reputation to consider. So has our young friend Groome. You'd better hand it over.'

'What?'

'Since you force me to be vulgar, whatever it was you were attempting to use as blackmail, my precious young friend,' he said.

'Whatever it may be, in fact, that you hold over young Groome and were trying to use in your attempt to force him to let you have a look at a confidential Government report concerning the orders which certain aircraft firms were likely to receive in the next six months. In your position you could have made pretty good use of them, couldn't you? Frankly, I haven't the faintest idea what this incriminating document may be. When I was young, objectionably wealthy youths accepted I.O.U.s from their poorer companions, but now that's gone out of fashion. What's the modern equivalent? An R.D. check, I suppose?'

Preen said nothing. He put his hand in an inner pocket and drew out an envelope which he handed over without a word. Campion examined the slip of pink paper within by the light of a pencil torch.

'You kept it for quite a time before trying to cash it, didn't you?' he said. 'Dear me, that's rather an old trick and it was never admired. Young men who are careless with their accounts have been caught out like that before. It simply wouldn't have looked good to his legal-minded old man, I take it? You two seem to be hampered by your respective papas' integrity. Yes, well, you can go now.'

Preen hesitated, opened his mouth to protest, but thought better of it. Lance looked after his retreating figure for some little time before he returned to his friend.

'Who wrote that blinking note?' he demanded.

'He did, of course,' said Campion brutally. 'He wanted to see the report but was making absolutely sure that young Groome took all the risks of being found with it.'

'Preen wrote the note,' Lance repeated blankly.

'Well, naturally,' said Campion absently. 'That was

obvious as soon as the report appeared in the picture. He was the only man in the place with the necessary special information to make use of it.'

Lance made no comment. He pulled his coat collar more closely about his throat and stuffed his hands into his pockets.

All the same the artist was not quite satisfied, for, later still, when Campion was sitting in his dressing-gown writing a note at one of the little escritoires which Florence so thoughtfully provided in her guest bedrooms, he came padding in again and stood warming himself before the fire.

'Why?' he demanded suddenly. 'Why did I get the invitation?'

'Oh, that was a question of luggage.' Campion spoke over his shoulder. 'That bothered me at first, but as soon as we fixed it on to Preen that little mystery became blindingly clear. Do you remember falling into the carriage this afternoon? Where did you put your elegant piece of gent's natty suitcasing? Over young Groome's head. Preen saw it from the corridor and assumed that the chap was sitting *under his own bag*! He sent his own man over here with the note, told him not to ask for Peter by name but to follow the nice new pigskin suitcase upstairs.'

Lance nodded regretfully. 'Very likely,' he said sadly. 'Funny thing. I was sure it was the girl.'

After a while he came over to the desk. Campion put down his pen and indicated the written sheet.

'Dear Groome,' it ran, 'I enclose a little matter that I should burn forthwith. The package you left in the inglenook is still there, right at the back on the left-hand side, cunningly concealed under a pile of logs. It has not been seen by anyone who could possibly understand it. If you nipped over very early this morning you could return it to its appointed place without any trouble. If I may venture a word of advice, it is never worth it.'

The author grimaced. 'It's a bit avuncular,' he admitted awkwardly, 'but what else can I do? His light is still on, poor chap. I thought I'd stick it under his door.'

Lance was grinning wickedly.

'That's fine,' he murmured. 'The old man does his stuff for reckless youth. There's just the signature now and that ought to be as obvious as everything else has been to you. I'll write it for you. "Merry Christmas. Love from Santa Claus."'

'You win,' said Mr Campion.

The Price of Light

Ellis Peters

Hamo FitzHamon of Lidyate held two fat manors in the north-eastern corner of the county, towards the border of Cheshire. Though a gross feeder, a heavy drinker, a self-indulgent lecher, a harsh landlord and a brutal master, he had reached the age of sixty in the best of health, and it came as a salutary shock to him when he was at last taken with a mild seizure, and for the first time in his life saw the next world yawning before him, and woke to the uneasy consciousness that it might see fit to treat him somewhat more austerely than this world had done. Though he re-pented none of them, he was aware of a whole register of acts in his past which heaven might construe as heavy sins. It began to seem to him a prudent precaution to acquire merit for his soul as quickly as possible. Also as cheaply, for he was a grasping and possessive man. A judicious gift to some holy house should secure the welfare of his soul. There was no need to go so far as endowing an abbey, or a new church of his own. The Benedictine abbey of Shrewsbury could put up a powerful assault of prayers on his behalf in return for a much more modest gift.

The thought of alms to the poor, however ostentatiously bestowed in the first place, did not recommend itself. Whatever was given would be soon consumed and forgotten, and a rag-tag of beggarly blessings from the indigent could carry very little weight, besides failing to confer a lasting lustre upon himself. No, he wanted something that would continue in daily use and daily respectful notice, a permanent reminder of his munificence and piety. He took his time about making his decision, and when he was satisfied of the best value he could get for the least expenditure, he sent his law-man to Shrewsbury to confer with abbot and prior, and conclude with due ceremony and many witnesses the charter that conveyed to the custodian of the altar of St Mary, within the abbey church, one of his free tenant farmers, the rent to provide light for Our Lady's altar throughout the year. He promised also, for the proper displaying of his charity, the gift of a pair of fine silver candlesticks, which he himself would bring and see installed on the altar at the coming Christmas feast.

Abbot Heribert, who after a long life of repeated

disillusionments still contrived to think the best of everybody, was moved to tears by this penitential generosity. Prior Robert, himself an aristocrat, refrained, out of Norman solidarity, from casting doubt upon Hamo's motive, but he elevated his eyebrows, all the same. Brother Cadfael, who knew only the public reputation of the donor, and was sceptical enough to suspend judgement until he encountered the source, said nothing, and waited to observe and decide for himself. Not that he expected much; he had been in the world fifty-five years, and learned to temper all his expectations, bad or good.

It was with mild and detached interest that he observed the arrival of the party from Lidyate, on the morning of Christmas Eve. A hard, cold Christmas it was proving to be, that year of 1135, all bitter black frost and grudging snow, thin and sharp as whips before a withering east wind. The weather had been vicious all the year, and the harvest a disaster. In the villages people shivered and starved, and Brother Oswald the almoner fretted and grieved the more that the alms he had to distribute were not enough to keep all those bodies and souls together. The sight of a cavalcade of three good riding horses, ridden by travellers richly wrapped up from the cold, and followed by two pack-ponies, brought all the wretched petitioners crowding and crying, holding out hands blue with frost. All they got out of it was a single perfunctory handful of small coin, and when they hampered his movements Fit-zHamon used his whip as a matter of course to clear the way. Rumour, thought Brother Cadfael, pausing on his way to the infirmary with his daily medicines for the sick, had probably not done Hamo FitzHamon any injustice.

Dismounting in the great court, the knight of Lidyate was seen to be a big, over-fleshed, top-heavy man with bushy hair and beard and eyebrows, all grey-streaked from their former black, and stiff and bristling as wire. He might well have been a very handsome man before indulgence purpled his face and pocked his skin and sank his sharp black eyes deep into flabby sacks of flesh. He looked more than his age, but still a man to be reckoned with.

The second horse carried his lady, pillion behind a groom. A small figure she made, even swathed almost to invisibility in her woollens and furs, and she rode snuggled comfortably against the groom's broad back, her arms hugging him round the waist. And a very well-looking young fellow he was, this groom, a strapping lad barely twenty years old, with round, ruddy cheeks and merry, guileless eyes, long in the legs, wide in the shoulders, everything a country youth should be, and attentive to his duties into the bargain, for he was down from the saddle in one lithe leap, and reaching up to take the lady by the waist, every bit as heartily as she had been clasping him a moment before, and lift her lightly down. Small, gloved hands rested on his shoulders a brief moment longer than was necessary. His respectful support of her continued until she was safe on the ground and sure of her footing; perhaps a few seconds more. Hamo FitzHamon was occupied with Prior Robert's ceremonious welcome, and the attentions of the hospitaller, who had made the best rooms of the guest-hall ready for him.

The third horse also carried two people, but the woman on the pillion did not wait for anyone to help her down, but slid quickly to the ground and hurried to help her mistress off with the great outer cloak in which she had travelled. A quiet, submissive young woman, perhaps in her middle twenties, perhaps older, in drab homespun, her hair hidden away under a coarse linen wimple. Her face was thin and pale, her skin dazzlingly fair, and her eyes, reserved and weary, were of a pale, clear blue, a fierce colour that ill suited their humility and resignation.

Lifting the heavy folds from her lady's shoulders, the maid showed a head the taller of the two, but drab indeed beside the bright little bird that emerged from the cloak. Lady FitzHamon came forth graciously smiling on the world in scarlet and brown, like a robin; and just as confidently. She had dark hair braided about a small, shapely head, soft, full cheeks flushed rosy by the chill air, and large dark eyes assured of their charm and power. She could not possibly have been more than thirty, probably not so much. FitzHamon had a grown son somewhere, with children of his own, and waiting, some said with little patience, for his inheritance. This girl must be a second or a third wife, a good deal younger than her stepson, and a beauty, at that. Hamo was secure enough and important enough to keep himself supplied with wives as he wore them out. This one must have cost him dear, for she had not the air of a poor but pretty relative sold for a profitable alliance, rather she looked as if she knew her own status very well indeed, and meant to have it acknowledged. She would look well presiding over the high table at Lidyate, certainly, which was probably the main consideration.

The groom behind whom the maid had ridden was an older man, lean and wiry, with a face like the bole of a knotty oak. By the sardonic patience of his eyes he had been in close and relatively favoured attendance on Fit-zHamon for many years, knew the best and the worst his moods could do, and was sure of his own ability to ride the storms. Without a word he set about unloading the pack-horses, and followed his lord to the guest-hall, while the young man took FitzHamon's bridle, and led the horses away to the stables.

Cadfael watched the two women cross to the doorway, the lady springy as a young hind, with bright eyes taking in everything around her, the tall maid keeping always a pace behind, with long steps curbed to keep her distance.

Even thus, frustrated like a mewed hawk, she had a graceful gait. Almost certainly of villein stock, like the two grooms. Cadfael had long practice in distinguishing the free from the unfree. Not that the free had any easy life, often they were worse off than the villeins of their neighbourhood; there were plenty of free men, this Christmas, gaunt and hungry, forced to hold out begging hands among the throng round the gatehouse. Freedom, the first ambition of every man, still could not fill the bellies of wives and children in a bad season.

FitzHamon and his party appeared at Vespers in full glory, to see the candlesticks reverently installed upon the altar in the Lady Chapel. Abbot, prior and brothers had no difficulty in sufficiently admiring the gift, for they were indeed things of beauty, two fluted stems ending in the twin cups of flowering lilies. Even the veins of the leaves showed delicate and perfect as in the living plant. Brother Oswald the almoner, himself a skilled silversmith when he had time to exercise his craft, stood gazing at the new embellishments of the altar with a face and mind curiously torn between rapture and regret, and ventured to delay the donor for a moment, as he was being ushered away to sup with Abbot Heribert in his lodging.

'My lord, these are of truly noble workmanship. I have some knowledge of precious metals, and of the most notable craftsmen in these parts, but I never saw any work so true to the plant as this. A country-man's eye is here, but the hand of a court craftsman. May we know who made them?'

FitzHamon's marred face curdled into deeper purple, as if an unpardonable shadow had been cast upon his hour of self-congratulation. He said brusquely: 'I commissioned them from a fellow in my own service. You would not know his name – a villein born, but he had some skill.' And with that he swept on, avoiding further question, and wife and men-servants and maid trailed after him. Only the older groom, who seemed less in awe of his lord than anyone, perhaps by reason of having so often presided over the ceremony of carrying him dead-drunk to his bed, turned back for a moment to pluck at Brother Oswald's sleeve, and advise him in a confidential whisper: 'You'll find him short to question on that head. The silversmith – Alard, his name was – cut and ran from his service last Christmas, and for all they hunted him as far as London, where the signs pointed, he's never been found. I'd let that matter lie, if I were you.'

And with that he trotted away after his master, and left several thoughtful faces staring after him.

'Not a man to part willingly with any property of his,' mused Brother Cadfael, 'metal or man, but for a price, and a steep price at that.'

'Brother, be ashamed!' reproved Brother Jerome at his

elbow. 'Has he not parted with these very treasures from pure charity?'

Cadfael refrained from elaborating on the profit Fitz-zHamon expected for his benevolence. It was never worth arguing with Jerome, who in any case knew as well as anyone that the silver lilies and the rent of one farm were no free gift. But Brother Oswald said grievingly: 'I wish he had directed his charity better. Surely these are beautiful things, a delight to the eyes, but well sold, they could have provided money enough to buy the means of keeping my poorest petitioners alive through the winter, some of whom will surely die for the want of them.'

Brother Jerome was scandalised. 'Has he not given them to Our Lady herself?' he lamented indignantly. 'Beware of the sin of those apostles who cried out with the same complaint against the woman who brought the pot of spikenard, and poured it over the Saviour's feet. Remember Our Lord's reproof to them, that they should let her alone, for she had done well!'

'Our Lord was acknowledging a well-meant impulse of devotion,' said Brother Oswald with spirit. 'He did not say it was well advised! "She hath done what she could" is what he said. He never said that with a little thought she might not have done better. What use would it have been to wound the giver, after the thing was done? Spilled oil of spikenard could hardly be recovered.'

His eyes dwelt with love and compunction upon the silver lilies, with their tall stems of wax and flame. For these remained, and to divert them to other use was still possible, or would have been possible if the donor had been a more approachable man. He had, after all, a right to dispose as he wished of his own property.

'It is sin,' admonished Jerome sanctimoniously, 'even to covet for other use, however worthy, that which has been given to Our Lady. The very thought is sin.'

'If Our Lady could make her own will known,' said Brother Cadfael drily, 'we might learn which is the graver sin, and which the more acceptable sacrifice.'

'Could any price be too high for the lighting of this holy altar?' demanded Jerome.

It was a good question, Cadfael thought, as they went to supper in the refectory. Ask Brother Jordan, for instance, the value of light. Jordan was old and frail, and gradually going blind. As yet he could distinguish shapes, but like shadows in a dream, though he knew his way about cloisters and precincts so well that his gathering darkness was no hindrance to his freedom of movement. But as every day the twilight closed in on him by a shade, so did his profound love of light grow daily more devoted, until he had forsaken other duties, and taken upon himself to tend all the lamps and candles on both altars, for the sake of being always irradiated by light, and sacred light, at that.

As soon as Compline was over, this evening, he would be busy devoutly trimming the wicks of candle and lamp, to have the steady flames smokeless and immaculate for the Matins of Christmas Day. Doubtful if he would go to his bed at all until Matins and Lauds were over. The very old need little sleep, and sleep is itself a kind of darkness. But what Jordan treasured was the flame of light, and not the vessel holding it; and would not those splendid two-pound candles shine upon him just as well from plain wooden sconces?

Cadfael was in the warming-house with the rest of the brothers, about a quarter of an hour before Compline, when a lay brother from the guest-hall came enquiring for him.

'The lady asks if you'll speak with her. She's complaining of a bad head, and that she'll never be able to sleep. Brother Hospitaller recommended her to you for a remedy.'

Cadfael went with him without comment, but with some curiosity, for at Vespers the Lady FitzHamon had looked in blooming health and sparkling spirits. Nor did she seem greatly changed when he met her in the hall, though she was still swathed in the cloak she had worn to cross the great court to and from the abbot's house, and had the hood so drawn that it shadowed her face. The silent maid hovered at her shoulder.

'You are Brother Cadfael? They tell me you are expert in herbs and medicines, and can certainly help me. I came early back from the lord abbot's supper, with such a headache, and have told my lord that I shall go early to bed. But I have such disturbed sleep, and with this pain how shall I be able to rest? Can you give me some draught that will ease me? They say you have a perfect apothecarium in your herb garden, and all your own work, growing, gathering, drying, brewing and all. There must be something there that can soothe pain and bring deep sleep.'

Well, thought Cadfael, small blame to her if she sometimes sought a means to ward off her old husband's rough attentions for a night, especially for a festival night when he was likely to have drunk heavily. Nor was it Cadfael's business to question whether the petitioner really needed his remedies. A guest might ask for whatever the house afforded.

'I have a syrup of my own making,' he said, 'which may do you good service. I'll bring you a vial of it from my workshop store.'

'May I come with you? I should like to see your workshop.' She had forgotten to sound frail and tired, the voice could have been a curious child's. 'As I already am cloaked and shod,' she said winningly. 'We just returned from the lord abbot's table.'

'But should you not go in from the cold, madam?

Though the snow's swept here in the court, it lies on some of the garden paths.'

'A few minutes in the fresh air will help me,' she said, 'before trying to sleep. And it cannot be far.'

It was not far. Once away from the subdued lights of the buildings they were aware of the stars, snapping like sparks from a cold fire, in a clear black sky just engendering a few tattered snow-clouds in the east. In the garden, between the pleached hedges, it seemed almost warm, as though the sleeping trees breathed tempered air as well as cutting off the bleak wind. The silence was profound. The herb garden was walled, and the wooden hut where Cadfael brewed and stored his medicines was sheltered from the worst of the cold. Once inside, and a small lamp kindled, Lady FitzHamon forgot her invalid role in wonder and delight, looking round her with bright, inquisitive eyes. The maid, submissive and still, scarcely turned her head, but her eyes ranged from left to right, and a faint colour touched life into her cheeks. The many faint, sweet scents made her nostrils quiver, and her lips curve just perceptibly with pleasure.

Curious as a cat, the lady probed into every sack and jar and box, peered at mortars and bottles, and asked a hundred questions in a breath.

'And this is rosemary, these little dried needles? And in this great sack – is it grain?' She plunged her hands wrist-deep inside the neck of it, and the hut was filled with sweetness. 'Lavender? Such a great harvest of it? Do you, then, prepare perfumes for us women?'

'Lavender has other good properties,' said Cadfael. He was filling a small vial with a clear syrup he made from eastern poppies, a legacy of his crusading years. 'It is helpful for all disorders that trouble the head and spirit, and its scent is calming. I'll give you a little pillow filled with that and other herbs, that shall help to bring you sleep. But this draught will ensure it. You may take all that I give you here, and get no harm, only a good night's rest.'

She had been playing inquisitively with a pile of small clay dishes he kept by his work-bench, rough dishes in which the fine seeds sifted from fruiting plants could be spread to dry out; but she came at once to gaze eagerly at the modest vial he presented to her. 'Is it enough? It takes much to give me sleep.'

'This,' he assured her patiently, 'would bring sleep to a strong man. But it will not harm even a delicate lady like you.'

She took it in her hand with a small, sleek smile of satisfaction. 'Then I thank you indeed! I will make a gift – shall I? – to your almoner in requital. Elfgiva, you bring the little pillow. I shall breathe it all night long. It should sweeten dreams.'

So her name was Elfgiva. A Norse name. She had Norse

eyes, as he had already noted, blue as ice, and pale, fine skin worn finer and whiter by weariness. All this time she had noted everything that passed, motionless, and never said word. Was she older, or younger, than her lady? There was no guessing. The one was so clamant, and the other so still.

He put out his lamp and closed the door, and led them back to the great court just in time to take leave of them and still be prompt for Compline. Clearly the lady had no intention of attending. As for the lord, he was just being helped away from the abbot's lodging, his grooms supporting him one on either side, though as yet he was not gravely drunk. They headed for the guest-hall at an easy roll. No doubt only the hour of Compline had concluded the drawn-out supper, probably to the abbot's considerable relief. He was no drinker, and could have very little in common with Hamo FitzHamon. Apart, of course, from a deep devotion to the altar of St Mary.

The lady and her maid had already vanished within the guest-hall. The younger groom carried in his free hand a large jug, full, to judge by the way he held it. The young wife could drain her draught and clutch her herbal pillow with confidence; the drinking was not yet at an end, and her sleep would be solitary and untroubled. Brother Cadfael went to Compline mildly sad, and obscurely comforted.

Only when service was ended, and the brothers on the

way to their beds, did he remember that he had left his flask of poppy syrup unstoppered. Not that it would come to any harm in the frosty night, but his sense of fitness drove him to go and remedy the omission before he slept.

His sandalled feet, muffled in strips of woollen cloth for warmth and safety on the frozen paths, made his coming quite silent, and he was already reaching out a hand to the latch of the door, but not yet touching, when he was brought up short and still by the murmur of voices within. Soft, whispering, dreamy voices that made sounds less and more than speech, caresses rather than words, though once at least words surfaced for a moment. A man's voice, young, wary, saying: 'But how if he *does* ... ?' And a woman's soft, suppressed laughter: 'He'll sleep till morning, never fear!' And her words were suddenly hushed with kissing, and her laughter became huge, ecstatic sighs; the young man's breath heaving triumphantly, but still, a moment later, the note of fear again, half-enjoyed: 'Still, you know him, he *may* ... ' And she, soothing: 'Not for an hour, at least ... then we'll go ... it will grow cold here ... '

That, at any rate, was true; small fear of them wishing to sleep out the night here, even two close-wrapped in one cloak on the bench-bed against the wooden wall. Brother Cadfael withdrew very circumspectly from the herb garden, and made his way back in chastened thought towards the dortoir. Now he knew who had swallowed that draught of his, and it was not the lady. In the pitcher of wine the young groom had been carrying? Enough for a strong man, even if he had not been drunk already. Meantime, no doubt, the body-servant was left to put his lord to bed, somewhere apart from the chamber where the lady lay supposedly nursing her indisposition and sleeping the sleep of the innocent. Ah, well, it was no business of Cadfael's, nor had he any intention of getting involved. He did not feel particularly censorious. Doubtful if she ever had any choice about marrying Hamo; and with this handsome boy for ever about them, to point the contrast … A brief experience of genuine passion, echoing old loves, pricked sharply through the years of his vocation. At least he knew what he was condoning. And who could help feeling some admiration for her opportunist daring, the quick wit that had procured the means, the alert eye that had seized on the most remote and adequate shelter available?

Cadfael went to bed, and slept without dreams, and rose at the Matin bell, some minutes before midnight. The procession of the brothers wound its way down the night stairs into the church, and into the soft, full glow of the lights before St Mary's altar.

Withdrawn reverently some yards from the step of the altar, old Brother Jordan, who should long ago have been in his cell with the rest, kneeled upright with clasped hands and ecstatic face, in which the great, veiled eyes stared full into the light he loved. When Prior Robert exclaimed in concern at finding him there on the stones, and laid a hand on his shoulder, he started as if out of a trance, and lifted to them a countenance itself all light.

'Oh, brothers, I have been so blessed! I have lived through a wonder … Praise God that ever it was granted to me! But bear with me, for I am forbidden to speak of it to any, for three days. On the third day from today I may speak … !'

'Look, brothers!' wailed Jerome suddenly, pointing. 'Look at the altar!'

Every man present, except Jordan, who still serenely prayed and smiled, turned to gape where Jerome pointed. The tall candles stood secured by drops of their own wax in two small clay dishes, such as Cadfael used for sorting seeds. The two silver lilies were gone from the place of honour.

Through loss, disorder, consternation, and suspicion, Prior Robert would still hold fast to the order of the day. Let Hamo FitzHamon sleep in happy ignorance till morning, still Matins and Lauds must be properly celebrated. Christmas was larger than all the giving and losing of silverware. Grimly he saw the services of the church observed, and despatched the brethren back to their beds until Prime, to sleep or lie wakeful and fearful, as they might. Nor would he allow any pestering of Brother Jerome by others, though possibly he did try in private to extort something more satisfactory from the old man. Clearly the theft, whether he knew anything about it or not, troubled Jordan not at all. To everything he said only: 'I am enjoined to silence until midnight of the third day.' And when they asked by whom? he smiled seraphically, and was silent.

It was Robert himself who broke the news to Hamo FitzHamon, in the morning, before Mass. The uproar, though vicious, was somewhat tempered by the after-effects of Cadfael's poppy draught, which dulled the edges of energy, if not of malice. His body-servant, the older groom Sweyn, was keeping well back out of reach, even with Robert still present, and the lady sat somewhat apart, too, as though still frail and possibly a little out of temper. She exclaimed dutifully, and apparently sincerely, at the outrage done to her husband, and echoed his demand that the thief should be hunted down, and the candlesticks recovered.

Prior Robert was just as zealous in the matter. No effort should be spared to regain the princely gift, of that they could be sure. He had already made certain of various circumstances which should limit the hunt. There had been a brief fall of snow after Compline, just enough to lay down a clean film of white on the ground. No single footprint had as yet marked this pure layer. He had only to look for himself at the paths leading from both parish doors of the church to see that no one had left by that way. The porter would swear that no one had passed the gatehouse; and on the one side of the abbey grounds not walled, the Meole brook was full and frozen, but the snow on both sides of it was virgin. Within the enclave, of course, tracks and cross-tracks were trodden out everywhere; but no one had left the enclave since Compline, when the candlesticks were still in their place.

'So the miscreant is still within the walls?' said Hamo, glinting vengefully. 'So much the better! Then his booty is still here within, too, and if we have to turn all your abode doors out of dortoirs, we'll find it! It, and him!'

'We will search everywhere,' agreed Robert, 'and question every man. We are as deeply offended as your lordship at this blasphemous crime. You may yourself oversee the search, if you will.'

So all that Christmas Day, alongside the solemn rejoicings in the church, an angry hunt raged about the precincts in full cry. It was not difficult for all the monks to account for their time to the last minute, their routine being so ordered that brother inevitably extricated brother from suspicion; and such as had special duties that took them out of the general view, like Cadfael in his visit to the herb garden, had all witnesses to vouch for them. The lay brothers ranged more freely, but tended to work in pairs, at least. The servants and the few guests protested their innocence, and if they had not, all of them, others willing to prove it, neither could Hamo prove the contrary. When it came to his own two grooms, there were several witnesses to testify that Sweyn had returned to his bed in the lofts of the stables as soon as he had put his lord to bed, and certainly empty-handed; and Sweyn, as Cadfael noted with interest, swore unblinkingly that young Madoc, who had come in an hour after him, had none the less returned with him, and spent that hour, at Sweyn's order, tending one of the pack-ponies, which showed signs of a cough, and that otherwise they had been together throughout.

A villein instinctively closing ranks with his kind against his lord? wondered Cadfael. Or does Sweyn know very well where that young man was last night, or at least what he was about, and is he intent on protecting him from a worse vengeance? No wonder Madoc looked a shade less merry and ruddy than usual this morning, though on the whole he kept his countenance very well, and refrained from even looking at the lady, while her tone to him was cool, sharp, and distant.

Cadfael left them hard at it again after the miserable meal they made of dinner, and went into the church alone. While they were feverishly searching every corner for the candlesticks he had forborne from taking part, but now they were elsewhere he might find something of interest there. He would not be looking for anything so obvious as two large silver candlesticks. He made obeisance at the altar, and mounted the step to look closely at the burning candles. No one had paid any attention to the modest containers that had been substituted for Hamo's gift, and just as well, in the circumstances, that Cadfael's workshop was very little visited, or these little clay pots might have been recognised as coming from there. He moulded and baked them himself as he wanted them. He had no intention of condoning theft, but neither did he relish the idea of any creature, however sinful, falling into Hamo FitzHamon's mercies.

Something long and fine, a thread of silver-gold, was caught and coiled in the wax at the base of one candle. Carefully he detached candle from holder, and unlaced from it a long, pale hair; to make sure of retaining it, he broke off the imprisoning disc of wax with it, and then hoisted and turned the candle to see if anything else was to be found under it. One tiny oval dot showed; with a fingernail he extracted a single seed of lavender. Left in the dish from beforetime? He thought not. The stacked pots were all empty. No, this had been brought here in the fold of a sleeve, most probably, and shaken out while the candle was being transferred.

The lady had plunged both hands with pleasure into the

sack of lavender, and moved freely about his workshop investigating everything. It would have been easy to take two of these dishes unseen, and wrap them in a fold of her cloak. Even more plausible, she might have delegated the task to young Madoc, when they crept away from their assignation. Supposing, say, they had reached the desperate point of planning flight together, and needed funds to set them on their way to some safe refuge ... yes, there were possibilities. In the meantime, the grain of lavender had given Cadfael another idea. And there was, of course, that long, fine hair, pale as flax, but brighter. The boy was fair. But so fair?

He went out through the frozen garden to his herbarium, shut himself securely into his workshop, and opened the sack of lavender, plunging both arms to the elbow and groping through the chill, smooth sweetness that parted and slid like grain. They were there, well down, his fingers traced the shape first of one, then a second. He sat down to consider what must be done.

Finding the lost valuables did not identify the thief. He could produce and restore them at once, but FitzHamon would certainly pursue the hunt vindictively until he found the culprit; and Cadfael had seen enough of him to know that it might cost life and all before this complainant was satisfied. He needed to know more before he would hand over any man to be done to death. Better not leave the things here, however. He doubted if they would ransack his hut, but they might. He rolled the candlesticks in a piece of sacking, and thrust them into the centre of the pleached hedge where it was thickest. The meagre, frozen snow had dropped with the brief sun. His arm went in to the shoulder, and when he withdrew it, the twigs sprang back and covered all, holding the package securely. Whoever had first hidden it would surely come by night to reclaim it, and show a human face at last.

It was well that he had moved it, for the searchers, driven by an increasingly angry Hamo, reached his hut before Vespers, examined everything within it, while he stood by to prevent actual damage to his medicines, and went away satisfied that what they were seeking was not there. They had not, in fact, been very thorough about the sack of lavender, the candlesticks might well have escaped notice even if he had left them there. It did not occur to anyone to tear the hedges apart, luckily. When they were gone, to probe all the fodder and grain in the barns, Cadfael restored the silver to its original place. Let the bait lie safe in the trap until the quarry came to claim it, as he surely would, once relieved of the fear that the hunters might find it first.

Cadfael kept watch that night. He had no difficulty in absenting himself from the dortoir, once everyone was in bed and asleep. His cell was by the night stairs, and the prior slept at the far end of the long room, and slept deeply. And bitter though the night air was, the sheltered hut was barely colder than his cell, and he kept blankets there for swathing some of his jars and bottles against frost. He took his little box with tinder and flint, and hid himself in the corner behind the door. It might be a wasted vigil; the thief, having survived one day, might think it politic to venture yet another before removing his spoils.

But it was not wasted. He reckoned it might be as late as ten o'clock when he heard a light hand at the door. Two hours before the bell would sound for Matins, almost two hours since the household had retired. Even the guest-hall should be silent and asleep by now; the hour was carefully chosen. Cadfael held his breath, and waited. The door swung open, a shadow stole past him, light steps felt their way unerringly to where the sack of lavender was propped against the wall. Equally silently Cadfael swung the door to again, and set his back against it. Only then did he strike a spark, and hold the blown flame to the wick of his little lamp.

She did not start or cry out, or try to rush past him and escape into the night. The attempt would not have succeeded, and she had had long practice in enduring what could not be cured. She stood facing him as the small flame steadied and burned taller, her face shadowed by the hood of her cloak, the candlesticks clasped possessively to her breast.

'Elfgiva!' said Brother Cadfael gently. And then: 'Are you here for yourself, or for your mistress?' But he thought he knew the answer already. That frivolous young wife would never really leave her rich husband and easy life, however tedious and unpleasant Hamo's attentions might be, to risk everything with her penniless villein lover. She would only keep him to enjoy in secret whenever she felt it safe. Even when the old man died she would submit to marriage at an overlord's will to another equally distasteful. She was not the stuff of which heroines and adventurers are made. This was another kind of woman.

Cadfael went close, and lifted a hand gently to put back the hood from her head. She was tall, a hand's-breadth taller than he, and erect as one of the lilies she clasped. The net that had covered her hair was drawn off with the hood, and a great flood of silver-gold streamed about her in the dim light, framing the pale face and startling blue eyes. Norse hair! The Danes had left their seed as far south as Cheshire, and planted this tall flower among them. She was no longer plain, tired and resigned. In this dim but loving light she shone in austere beauty. Just so must Brother Jordan's veiled eyes have seen her.

'Now I see!' said Cadfael. 'You came into the Lady Chapel, and shone upon our half-blind brother's darkness as you shine here. You are the visitation that brought him awe and bliss, and enjoined silence upon him for three days.'

The voice he had scarcely heard speak a word until then, a voice level, low and beautiful, said: 'I made no claim to be what I am not. It was he who mistook me. I did not refuse the gift.'

'I understand. You had not thought to find anyone there, he took you by surprise as you took him. He took you for Our Lady herself, disposing as she saw fit of what had been given her. And you made him promise you three days' grace.' The lady had plunged her hands into the sack, yes, but Elfgiva had carried the pillow, and a grain or two had filtered through the muslin to betray her.

'Yes,' she said, watching him with unwavering blue eyes.

'So in the end you had nothing against him making known how the candlesticks were stolen.' It was not an accusation, he was pursuing his way to understanding.

But at once she said clearly: 'I did not steal them. I took them. I will restore them – to their owner.'

'Then you don't claim they are yours?'

'No,' she said, 'they are not mine. But neither are they FitzHamon's.'

'Do you tell me,' said Cadfael mildly, 'that there has been no theft at all?'

269

'Oh, yes,' said Elfgiva, and her pallor burned into a fierce brightness, and her voice vibrated like a harp-string. 'Yes, there has been a theft, and a vile, cruel theft, too, but not here, not now. The theft was a year ago, when FitzHamon received these candlesticks from Alard who made them, his villein, like me. Do you know what the promised price was for these? Manumission for Alard, and marriage with me, what we had begged of him three years and more. Even in villeinage we would have married and been thankful. But he promised freedom! Free man makes free wife, and I was promised, too. But when he got the fine works he wanted, then he refused the promised price. He laughed! I saw, I heard him! He kicked Alard away from him like a dog. So what was his due, and denied him, Alard took. He ran! On St Stephen's Day he ran!'

'And left you behind?' said Cadfael gently.

'What chance had he to take me? Or even to bid me farewell? He was thrust out to manual labour on FitzHamon's other manor. When his chance came, he took it and fled. I was not sad! I rejoiced! Whether I live or die, whether he remembers or forgets me, he is free. No, but in two days more he will be free. For a year and a day he will have been working for his living in his own craft, in a charter borough, and after that he cannot be haled back into servitude, even if they find him.'

'I do not think,' said Brother Cadfael, 'that he will

have forgotten you! Now I see why our brother may speak after three days. It will be too late then to try to reclaim a runaway serf. And you hold that these exquisite things you are cradling belong by right to Alard who made them?'

'Surely,' she said, 'seeing he never was paid for them, they are still his.'

'And you are setting out tonight to take them to him. Yes! As I heard it, they had some cause to pursue him towards London ... indeed, into London, though they never found him. Have you had better word of him? *From* him?'

The pale face smiled. 'Neither he nor I can read or write. And whom should he trust to carry word until his time is complete, and he is free? No, never any word.'

'But Shrewsbury is also a charter borough, where the unfree may work their way to freedom in a year and a day. And sensible boroughs encourage the coming of good craftsmen, and will go far to hide and protect them. I know! So you think he may be here. And the trail towards London a false trail. True, why should he run so far, when there's help so near? But, daughter, what if you do not find him in Shrewsbury?'

'Then I will look for him elsewhere until I do. I can live as a runaway, too, I have skills, I can make my own way until I do get word of him. Shrewsbury can as well make room for a good seamstress as for a man's gifts, and someone in the silversmith's craft will know where to find a brother so talented as Alard. I shall find him!'

'And when you do? Oh, child, have you looked beyond that?'

'To the very end,' said Elfgiva firmly. 'If I find him and he no longer wants me, no longer thinks of me, if he is married and has put me out of his mind, then I will deliver him these things that belong to him, to do with as he pleases, and go my own way and make my own life as best I may without him. And wish well to him as long as I live.'

Oh, no, small fear, she would not be easily forgotten, not in a year, not in many years. 'And if he is utterly glad of you, and loves you still?'

'Then,' she said, gravely smiling, 'if he is of the same mind as I, I have made a vow to Our Lady, who lent me her semblance in the old man's eyes, that we will sell these candlesticks where they may fetch their proper price, and that price shall be delivered to your almoner to feed the hungry. And that will be our gift, Alard's and mine, though no one will ever know it.'

'Our Lady will know it,' said Cadfael, 'and so shall I. Now, how were you planning to get out of this enclave and into Shrewsbury? Both our gates and the town gates are closed until morning.'

She lifted eloquent shoulders. 'The parish doors are not

barred. And even if I leave tracks, will it matter, provided I find a safe hiding-place inside the town?'

'And wait in the cold of the night? You would freeze before morning. No, let me think. We can do better for you than that.'

Her lips shaped: "*We?*" in silence, wondering, but quick to understand. She did not question his decisions, as he had not questioned hers. He thought he would long remember the slow, deepening smile, the glow of warmth mantling her cheeks. 'You believe me!' she said.

'Every word! Here, give me the candlesticks, let me wrap them, and do you put up your hair again in net and hood. We've had no fresh snow since morning, the path to the parish door is well trodden, no one will know your tracks among the many. And, girl, when you come to the town end of the bridge there's a little house off to the left, under the wall, close to the town gate. Knock there and ask for shelter over the night till the gates open, and say that Brother Cadfael sent you. They know me, I doctored their son when he was sick. They'll give you a warm corner and a place to lie, for kindness' sake, and ask no questions, and answer none from others, either. And likely they'll know where to find the silversmiths of the town, to set you on your way.'

She bound up her pale, bright hair and covered her head, wrapping the cloak about her, and was again the maidservant in homespun. She obeyed without question his every word, moved silently at his back round the great court by way of the shadows, halting when he halted, and so he brought her to the church, and let her out by the parish door into the public street, still a good hour before Matins. At the last moment she said, close at his shoulder within the half-open door: 'I shall be grateful always. Some day I shall send you word.'

'No need for words,' said Brother Cadfael, 'if you send me the sign I shall be waiting for. Go now, quickly, there's not a soul stirring.'

She was gone, lightly and silently, flitting past the abbey gatehouse like a tall shadow, towards the bridge and the town. Cadfael closed the door softly, and went back up the night stairs to the dortoir, too late to sleep, but in good time to rise at the sound of the bell, and return in procession to celebrate Matins.

There was, of course, the resultant uproar to face next morning, and he could not afford to avoid it, there was too much at stake. Lady FitzHamon naturally expected her maid to be in attendance as soon as she opened her eyes, and raised a petulant outcry when there was no submissive shadow waiting to dress her and do her hair. Calling failed to summon and search to find Elfgiva, but it was an hour or more before it dawned on the lady that she had lost her accomplished maid for good. Furiously she made her own toilet, unassisted, and raged out to complain to her husband, who had risen before her, and was waiting for her to accompany him to Mass. At her angry declaration that Elfgiva was nowhere to be found, and must have run away during the night, he first scoffed, for why should a sane girl take herself off into a killing frost when she had warmth and shelter and enough to eat where she was? Then he made the inevitable connection, and let out a roar of rage.

'Gone, is she? And my candlesticks gone with her, I dare swear! So it was *she*! The foul little thief! But I'll have her yet, I'll drag her back, she shall not live to enjoy her ill-gotten gains ... '

It seemed likely that the lady would heartily endorse all this; her mouth was already open to echo him when Brother Cadfael, brushing her sleeve close as the agitated brothers ringed the pair, contrived to shake a few grains of lavender on to her wrist. Her mouth closed abruptly. She gazed at the tiny things for the briefest instant before she shook them off, she flashed an even briefer glance at Brother Cadfael, caught his eye, and heard in a rapid whisper: 'Madam, softly! – proof of the maid's innocence is also proof of the mistress's.'

She was by no means a stupid woman. A second quick glance confirmed what she had already grasped, that there was one man here who had a weapon to hold over her at least as deadly as any she could use against Elfgiva. She was also a woman of decision, and wasted no time in bitterness once her course was chosen. The tone in which she addressed her lord was almost as sharp as that in which she had complained of Elfgiva's desertion.

'She your thief, indeed! That's folly, as you should very well know. The girl is an ungrateful fool to leave me, but a thief she never has been, and certainly is not this time. She can't possibly have taken the candlesticks, you know well enough when they vanished, and you know I was not well that night, and went early to bed. She was with me until long after Brother Prior discovered the theft. I asked her to stay with me until you came to bed. *As you never did!*' she ended tartly. 'You may remember!'

Hamo probably remembered very little of that night; certainly he was in no position to gainsay what his wife so roundly declared. He took out a little of his ill-temper on her, but she was not so much in awe of him that she dared not reply in kind. Of course she was certain of what she said! *She* had not drunk herself stupid at the lord abbot's table, she had been nursing a bad head of another kind, and even with Brother Cadfael's remedies she had not slept until after midnight, and Elfgiva had then been still beside her. Let him hunt a runaway maidservant, by all means, the thankless hussy, but never call her a thief, for she was none.

Hunt her he did, though with less energy now it seemed clear he would not recapture his property with her. He sent his grooms and half the lay servants off in both directions to enquire if anyone had seen a solitary girl in a hurry; they were kept at it all day, but they returned empty-handed.

The party from Lidyate, less one member, left for home next day. Lady FitzHamon rode demurely behind young Madoc, her cheek against his broad shoulders; she even gave Brother Cadfael the flicker of a conspiratorial smile as the cavalcade rode out of the gates, and detached one arm from round Madoc's waist to wave as they reached the roadway. So Hamo was not present to hear when Brother Jordan, at last released from his vow, told how Our Lady had appeared to him in a vision of light, fair as an angel, and taken away with her the candlesticks that were hers to take and do with as she would, and how she had spoken to him, and enjoined on him his three days of silence. And if there were some among the listeners who wondered whether the fair woman had not been a more corporeal being, no one had the heart to say so to Jordan, whose vision was comfort and consolation for the fading of the light.

That was at Matins, at midnight of the day of St Stephen's. Among the scattering of alms handed in at the gatehouse next morning for the beggars, there was a little basket that weighed surprisingly heavily. The porter could not remember who had brought it, taking it to be some offerings of food or old clothing, like all the rest; but when it was opened it sent Brother Oswald, almost incoherent with joy and wonder, running to Abbot Heribert to report what seemed to be a miracle. For the basket was full of gold coin, to the value of more than a hundred marks. Well used, it would ease all the worst needs of his poorest petitioners, until the weather relented.

'Surely,' said Brother Oswald devoutly, 'Our Lady has made her own will known. Is not this the sign we have hoped for?'

Certainly it was for Cadfael, and earlier than he had dared to hope for it. He had the message that needed no words. She had found him, and been welcomed with joy. Since midnight Alard the silversmith had been a free man, and free man makes free wife. Presented with such a woman as Elfgiva, he could give as gladly as she, for what was gold, what was silver, by comparison?